SECRET OF CERES BOOK 4

Zenith

STELLA WILLIAMS

Zenith: Secret of Ceres Book 4

Print ISBN: 978-1-7347301-9-7
Ebook ISBN: 978-1-7347301-8-0

Editing
Raw Book Editing
www.rawbookediting.com

Book Cover Design
RebeccaCovers on Fiverr

Published by
Serpentine Creative LLC
www.serpentinecreative.com

For all the women who
exemplify Black Girl Magic

Prologue

Pitch black with not a single star in the sky. Heavy clouds hung low and ominous, like thick, wet blankets ready to relieve the weight of the water they carried all over the city and wash away the day.

Zazzie sat alone on her porch naked, except for the handwoven shawl draped over her shoulders. She had intended to moon-bathe, but it appeared that wasn't the cleansing the universe had in store for her.

Zazzie lit the coals under her frankincense resin and watched as the black disks glowed red before turning ash white, billows of smoke rose to join the cloudy sky above. She dropped her shawl, standing over her ceremonial bowl, and proceeded with her cleansing ritual.

After this week, she needed a fresh start. She needed guidance from her ancestors and from the goddess within. She chanted her affirmations. Her body swayed to its own rhythm. Her heart beat in her chest, the loud thrum like a drum sounding to the beat she raised her voice to sing.

She rubbed her naked belly just below her navel, caressing her womb and asking forgiveness for letting herself go so long without letting her speak.

A crash of thunder. A bright streak of lightning

danced across the sky. Briefly lighting the ground beneath Zazzie's feet. Electricity crackled in the air. The tiny hairs on her arms rose to meet it.

Breathe…2…3…4.   Hold…2…3…4. Release…2…3…4.

A fat, wet droplet slapped against her cheek before trailing down her face, a tear from heaven. Then the clouds released, a blanket of water splashed around her, coating her skin, cleansing her body. She wept, the salted warmth mixing with the icy droplets.

Zazzie crouched down, sitting back on her heels. She turned her head up to the sky, opened her mouth wide, and screamed. She didn't care if she bothered her neighbors, most would be sleeping at this hour, and the driving rain would drown out the deep guttural tone that escaped her.

She sank into the sopping wet grass, her toes slipping in the mud beneath. She closed her eyes and focused on her breath. Concentrated on the energy of the earth beneath her and the sky above her. She became one with her surroundings. Relaxing into the current. Until the weight of the negative energy she'd been carrying fell from her body. Lighting struck the ground, mere inches from her. If her eyes weren't already closed, she would have been blinded by the brilliant light. The electricity traveled through the wet ground, branching into her body; white-hot light seized her. The power of nature coursed through her, transferring her consciousness to a plane beyond the physical.

Zarovia

The soft whisper tickled her ear. She was blind, but she wasn't afraid, nor was she alone. She could feel the energy of others around her, powerful energies.

Zarovia

She reached out with her hands. She could feel their

presence but could not make contact with them. Not in a tangible way.

We are here to guide you.

She felt a force urging her forward. Carefully, she took one step, then another. With each step she took, her vision cleared. She studied her surroundings as they were revealed to her. It was dark and cold. Steel gray walls, not quite stone, not quite metal, rose in a great dome around her. The room was circular in the center, an altar of sorts. It wasn't like any altar she had ever seen. Intricate carvings glowed with purple energy like the entrance of Ceres once did.

She crept forward, stopping just before the altar. In the middle was a handprint.

Don't be afraid. You have been chosen.

The voice bounced around the room. Zazzie turned around but could see nothing more than the strange dome. There was no entrance or exit. She turned back to the altar. An unseen force guided her hand to the imprint in the stone. It was smooth and warm to the touch. Her hand sank into the stone, gentle suction like quicksand as the hard surface morphed into something else entirely—the tiny particles glowing with aubergine wonder. Needles of fear pricked at her skin. She attempted to pull free, but it was no use. She was elbow deep in whatever this altar or organism was. She couldn't be entirely sure it wasn't a living entity as it pulsated with energies unfamiliar to anything Zazzie had ever encountered.

Do you accept your calling?

The disembodied voice had returned. It was only then that Zazzie realized it was in her head. Someone with powerful mind energies was obviously playing tricks on her. There was only one person she knew who was strong enough and immature enough to do such a thing.

"Jaquis Andromeda! Get out of my head!"

Her yell echoed around the chamber.

Do you accept your calling?

"What calling?"

Zazzie had no idea why she spoke out loud to a voice in her head. If this really was Jaq's doing, she would kick his behind up and down the streets of Langsmith for this foolishness.

Do you accept?

Frustrated, Zazzie closed her eyes and focused on kicking whoever was messing with her out of her head. Now was not the time for tricks like this. If this was indeed Jaq, he needed to be saving this kind of energy for the trials that lay ahead. He was on the Ruling Council now. He should have more respect for his duties and the title. Then again, Jaq had never held the Ruling Council in any sort of regard.

Her strain made no difference. While she still felt the energies flowing around her, Zazzie had no access to them. Further evidence that it was all some sick, twisted mind fuck of a dream. Maybe it was all just some shitty psychosis triggered by everything that had happened over the last few months.

Finding out the Aura were being hunted by Vampires for their blood was enough to give any Aura nightmares. Learning that one of their own had worked with such monsters and brought about not only the death of a respected leader in the Aura community but the fall of the Great Sanctuary of Ceres itself was devastating. It was a wonder any Aura had the will to continue with the lack of structure and socialization that would help her people flourish in this new world.

Zazzie had a vision, and yet no one seemed willing to help her. The odds were stacked against her, but she would not rest until she saw it through. She would have to be as ferocious as Farrah to convince the others of the importance of her work. As dauntless as Disrayan in seeing it through, and as earnest as Enora in her efforts to ensure her people's future.

An eerie calm settled over the space. The grip on her arm loosened, and Zarovia was able to pull her hand free. Now free from its hold, she realized there was something in her hand, a stone object. She held it up to get a better look at it. It was like no other stone she had ever seen. It was light as a feather, yet seemed to have its own gravity to it. The energy pulsing from its core felt so pure and undiluted, it stung to hold.

You have accepted your calling. You are the keeper of your people's past, present, and future—the Zenith.

Zarovia opened her mouth to ask what that was supposed to mean, but before she could get the words out, the room exploded with light. Pain like she had never experienced before racked every inch of her body. Images flashed before her eyes—the past, present, and future of her people—and then she understood. She truly understood. This was the Zenith; she was the Zenith. Her body convulsed; her brain overloaded with so much information in such a short time.

All she could do was close her eyes and pray she would have the strength to do as the ancestors demanded of her.

Spark

Golden candelabras hung menacingly overhead, their weight straining the delicate chains holding them in position. The soft flickering of lit candles set the stage for the ominous discussion ahead; four thrones placed in a circle around the room. There was no table or material for taking notes. The Vampire Council had no higher authority to report to. The so-called Royal line were mostly figureheads. Only apprised of the Council's decisions by their appointed representative, the late Maximus. It was the first meeting of the Vampire Council since the death of Maximus

Most considered his passing a tragedy. Kirima wasn't most. In fact, she would be happy the bastard was dead if it wasn't for the massive power vacuum left in his wake. A Council position was open for the first time in centuries. That meant every Vampire with ties to the Royal line were vying for it. Barely respectful, underhushed whispers and side conversations as not to offend the man's daughter temporarily in his place. Kirima had waded through the hopefuls on her way to the meeting chambers.

Kirima nodded at Carrie. She seemed as thrilled to be there as the rest of the Council appeared to be. A woman on the Council wasn't to the liking of Vampire men. Patriarchy was still alive and well in Vampire society. Kirima was only tolerated because of her undeniable record as a warrior for the race. She was the last of her kind, part of the Vampire element amongst the great Moors who conquered Africa and Europe. Her dark skin and thick build were more than just elements of beauty to be admired.

Carrie was the exact opposite. She was everything these men felt a born Vampire female should be—thin, pale, soft-spoken, and all-around unassuming. She looked shrunken and fragile in her father's thrown. A child amongst titans. The only show of force, the mysterious man who stood as her guard. The others might not recognize the man's importance, but Kirima did. He'd been part of Maura's retinue. Kirima knew the dark aura because one of her own men had once been victim to that monster. Curious, considering it was one of Maura's changelings who had killed her beloved father.

Kirima took her seat after nodding to her fellow Council members.

"Let's get this over with, shall we?" she said.

Cadmael sat up straight, leaning away from his brother Eadrich.

"Yes, I have more pressing issues to attend to."

"More pressing matters, really?" Nathaniel scoffed, tugging at the sleeves of his black suit jacket.

"Yes," Eadrich answered. "Now, if we can just move this along."

Nathaniel rolled his eyes and signaled with his finger for Carrie to speak.

She bit her lip nervously before glancing at her guard, who gave her a reassuring nod.

"My father's death was tragic, but I have come to forgive those who made it happen. Not because I feel my father's death was justified, but I understand their position. My father was acting against the interests of Vampire society. He was trafficking in humans and others."

Kirima watched the other members of the Council for their reactions. They were not surprised by this new information. Kirima quickly realized she was the one out of the loop.

"Carrie, my dear, those are simply rumors. You know our kind doesn't deal in the black-market blood trade. That is for those on the fringe," Nathaniel said.

Carrie stiffened as if stricken by his words.

After the meeting, Kirima would make it a point to get the full story. Of course, she had received the briefing prepared by Brody. Maximus's right hand, who was miraculously the only one to survive both attacks. No matter what Carrie's answer was to the questions Kirima had for her, it wouldn't matter. The men had already made up their minds. It was now an all-out war in Langsmith. No one was safe.

Not even the Council members, as had become evident with Maximus's death in his own compound. It was why Kirima had sent her daughter away. On top of the threat from Langsmith, those vying for the Council position would likely target her daughter, Aliridon, to gain favor. Aliridon wasn't ready to mate. Kirima had no intention of forcing her or allowing her to be forced into mating either.

Carrie wasn't going to be immune to the prospect of forced marriage. While that didn't sit right with Kirima either, it wasn't her place or in her best interest to interfere in that regard. No, Kirima would wait until she saw the whole picture. There were too many unanswered questions that didn't sit right with her, and Kirima would not let the arrogant assholes who sat beside her have the upper hand.

"Thank you for sharing your opinion, Carrie. I believe that is all we require of you at the moment. The Council has much to discuss, and I am sure you are anxious to get back to your mourning."

Carrie's eyes fluttered closed, and she took a deep breath before opening them again. A fire danced there that hadn't been there before. Kirima couldn't help but smirk. Maybe the female wasn't as docile and useless as they thought.

"It is not an opinion. It is a fact. I loved my father, but he was hardly a man anyone cared to aspire to be. The people of Langsmith were acting in self-defense above all else. It is a tragedy, yes, but they don't deserve our ire. At least, not for this."

Carrie was half out of the thrown by the end of her speech. The room was deathly silent before Nathaniel leaned forward, a dangerous glint in his eye.

"Young lady, it is not your decision who deserves punishment for this act. It wasn't just the death of a Council member. It was an attack on the original families, the Vampire race as a whole. You've been slumming it for far too long. Your judgment has been tainted by undesirables. Leave us before our respect for your father is outweighed by your insolence."

Carrie's guard moved stealthily but not quick enough. His outstretched hand was just in range to wrap thick fingers around Nathaniel's throat before Nathaniel's guard intercepted him. It became clear this would go south quickly, and Kirima did not want to see blood shed this evening.

"Enough!" Her voice rang from every corner of the room. Everyone froze.

"This is not the time, nor the place, for this. Carrie, please leave and take your pet with you," she snapped.

The guards didn't look like they would let the man go, but eventually, they released him with a not-so-gentle shove toward Carrie.

Carrie rushed to her guard, and for a moment, Kirima noticed a spark between the two. Maybe their relationship was more than just employer, employee.

"This isn't over," Carrie hissed before they both left the room. Kirima sat back equal parts relieved and perturbed.

***

Zarovia did her best to focus on her work, instead of the intensity of last night. Between the ancestor's message and the insane sexual energy it had left her with, last night had been more exhausting than all of the previous month's emergencies combined. She was finally focused on something other than the Zenith and the feel of Hendrex inside of her when there was a knock on the door frame to her office.

"Can I help you?" Zarovia didn't look up from the stack of papers in front of her. She had slacked off on her reports last week with everything that had occurred with Ceres and the Aura, but now her human life had forced itself back to the forefront.

Working with children was a blessing and a curse. Zazzie saw a little bit of everything when it came to Langsmith Public Schools' students. The town was pretty big, but the number of children was small enough to only warrant two schools. The district could only afford one counselor for both. That meant, while she had an office at each school, her main office was in the school board office building, and that left her office open to a lot of unwanted intrusions, like right then.

"You haven't returned my calls." Derrick Laughton stood leaning against the door frame.

He stared at her with deep brown eyes and licked his lips like he wanted a taste of her. She'd given him a taste once, right before things got crazy with Ceres and Hendrex finally made his move on her. In the chaos of everything, she hadn't had a chance to really let Derrick off the hook. Had been avoiding it, actually. Her mind had been preoccupied with more important things. He pushed off the door frame and moved to close the door. Zazzie frowned and forced herself to look up from her work.

"I've been busy, but since you are here now, I am not interested in continuing our non-working situation," she said and focused back on her work.

Derrick sucked his teeth and leaned on her desk.

"You sure about that?" His hand moved to touch one of her locs that had fallen from where she'd twisted it into a crown on top of her head.

She leaned her head away and shot daggers in his direction.

"I am quite sure."

He shook his head and tucked his hand into the pocket of his tan slacks.

"And people wonder why black women stay single."

Zarovia bit the inside of her cheek to keep from cussing the man out and forced a smile on her face.

"Well, with the invention of the dildo, limp dick men just don't make the cut."

She lifted her hand and waved him away. Derrick bared his teeth at her, but before he could come up with another disgusting retort, Sheila from down the hall knocked on the door and opened it.

"Sorry to interrupt, Ms. Monoceros, but there are students here to see you."

"Send them in." Zarovia was glad for the disruption, but at the same time, her spider senses tingled.

A student making the trek to her office during school hours wasn't the norm and couldn't be anything good. Sure enough, Daphne Orion paraded into her office. The girl's clothing was disheveled, and she sported a busted lip. Next to her stood Sarah Greywulf, the young Shifter who worked as a part-time spy for the Langsmith Shifter pack and Tyr Greywulf's adopted daughter. Neither girl looked happy, and they checked to make sure Sheila and Derrick were long gone before the tense set of their shoulders relaxed.

"Why aren't you two in school?"

"I caught this one picking fights with Vampire minions," Sarah said, pointing at Daphne.

Daphne hung her head but didn't speak.

"Ms. Orion, I know things have been hard for you since the incident, but that doesn't mean you go looking for trouble."

Daphne's head came up, fire danced in her eyes, and the temperature in the room shot up a good ten degrees.

"They attacked me first!"

"After you called them fangbangers," Sarah replied.

Daphne turned her ire on Sarah.

"That's what they are, mangy mutt."

Sarah squared her shoulders, her eyes flashing yellow, the irises turning to feline slits.

"Keep talking, Glow worm."

"Enough!" Zarovia said, using her own energy to hold the two teenagers in place. She couldn't have them fighting in her office. Especially with the display of energy Daphne had just shown. It was more than her parents had noted in her files. It made Zarovia wonder if Daphne was one of the Auraless whose power had increased after the surge. It was affecting teens and young children more than adults if the reports and rumors were accurate. "Sit down while I call your parents."

"Like they will do anything but try to hide me away," Daphne spat.

Zarovia frowned and set the phone down.

"What do you mean by that?"

"After the incident, when I was returned to them. At first, it was fine. They were happy I was home, but then the blame game started. My dad blamed my mom for not having enough energy in her family line to provide him with strong children. If we were stronger, they could have stayed in Ceres, where I would have been safe. My mom blamed my father for being too strict about teaching us Aura knowledge. If I knew the dangers, I never would have been stupid enough to run off with The Resistance."

"I'm sure they are just dealing with the trauma of almost losing you. Maybe I can speak with them," Zarovia offered.

"It's no use. At the end of the day, it's all my fault. I trusted James. I went off alone with him. I got kidnapped because I wasn't strong enough. Not as an Aura, and not as a human. Not anymore, though. I am more powerful now. I can feel it. So, why not use it to keep others from making my same mistakes? Calling out fangbangers is the least I could do."

Sarah snorted and shook her head.

"You mean, getting the crap kicked out of you by fangbangers. Doesn't matter if you are strong in energy if you have no idea how to wield it to your advantage," Sarah said.

"Says the girl who almost knocked me out with her own energy shield," Daphne muttered.

Zarovia sat up straighter.

"What do you mean she almost knocked you out?"

Sarah suddenly seemed uncomfortable.

"I think I'll head back to the compound now," she said and stood to leave.

Zarovia focused her energy to pull the girl back down into her seat.

"Not so fast. Tell me what is going on with you."

Fear crept into the girl's eyes. "Please don't tell Tyr."

"Don't tell him what?"

"Ever since the energy blast, I've discovered I can feel things differently."

"Differently how?"

"I can feel and distinguish the energy of things. I haven't really explored it until today, and that was by accident. I saw Daphne in trouble, and before I could even react, I felt the energy shooting from me in a wave. It knocked out her attackers and knocked her down as well."

Zarovia blinked a few times before shaking her head. She didn't know Sarah's story, other than she had been abandoned by her original pack and adopted by Tyr years later. Maybe the reason she was abandoned was what some Shifters would consider a tainted lineage.

"I have to tell him something, but I promise not to divulge your secret yet. I think you should be the one to tell him. As for you, Daphne, I can't just let this go. Not only do you need to learn to control your new energy, but you need help coping with what happened to you. Now, in place of detention for skipping class today, I will do you a favor this once, but both of you have to agree to after-school lessons with me."

"Lessons? On what?" Daphne said.

"Both of you need guidance in controlling your energy, and frankly, if you are going to insist on fighting, you need to learn how to properly defend yourself. So, from now on, we will meet once a week at the Factory. I will teach you both how to use your energy abilities properly, and Sarah, you can teach Daphne how to protect herself."

Neither girl looked pleased with the idea, but on this, Zarovia wasn't budging. It was plain to see they both needed help and also a friend to go through it with. There was an awkward silence between them all before each girl looked at each other and nodded.

"Fine, but this doesn't make me any less Shifter," Sarah grumbled.

"No one implied any different," Zarovia assured her before picking up her phone to dial the girl's parents.

"I thought you were letting us off," Daphne said.

Zarovia smiled.

"From detention, not from calling your parents."

Both girls groaned and sank into their chairs as Zarovia made the necessary calls. Zazzie's hands trembled as she finalized plans to meet with Sarah and Daphne's guardians. It wasn't like she was nervous about calling a student's parents. That was sixty percent of her job. No, her hands trembled because this was it, the start of her duties as Zenith. The catalyst for major change. She knew the ancestor's plan but hadn't expected things to start immediately. Her destiny was to provide a path for the future of the Aura, and for Zazzie, that meant the school she'd been dreaming of for years, among other things. Here she was, getting ready to take on her very first students. *If* she could get their parents to agree.

The calls were thankfully brief. Zazzie would meet with the two female guardians tomorrow afternoon. If only that were the end of her duties. The work day was far from over for her, but her anxiety would make the rest of the day a slog. At least she had something to look forward to at the end of her days now. Having Hendrex around was an adjustment, but she was starting to like the domestic routine they had settled into.

***

Hendrex let his eyes flutter open. The small candle he lit for his morning meditation had burned out. It was the smell of smoke in the air that had brought him out of his Zen state.

He reached for his journal, one of the few things he managed to save when Ceres fell. Its brown leather binding was soft and comforting in his palm. He cracked open the tan parchment to a new page, quickly catching the ballpoint pen that rolled out of it. Holding the thin plastic tube between his fingers didn't give him the same sense of accomplishment writing with his quill and ink had. Still, he could appreciate the smooth flow of the modern writing device. He carefully penned the details from his latest attempt at connecting with the ancestral plane with a sigh.

He'd made more progress today than he had since the fall of Ceres. Maybe he'd lost more than just his position on the Ruling Council. Perhaps, the ancestors also deemed him unworthy.

Hendrex pushed the thoughts away and recorded where he had encountered resistance on his metaphysical journey. He was still able to transcend his physical self. He was able to connect with the turbulent energy that coursed through Langsmith. Yet, when he reached further, tried to go beyond the city limits or beyond the mortal plane, he'd been met with resistance. No, a rejection that sent him plummeting back to his physical form.

Maybe they were trying to tell him he needed to focus on what was in front of him and not what was above him. He had no idea what the significance of that could be. Did it have something to do with what was to come for the Aura? Had he truly failed them in the mission he'd been given before being removed from the Ruling Council? He shuddered at the thought. The ancestors had shown him a dark and fiery end to his people if he didn't meet their goals.

Yet, hadn't that been exactly what happened? Hendrex failed the Aura, and now their Sanctuary was gone.

No, the fall of Ceres had been inevitable, but he couldn't help but wonder if his actions had sped up the process. Hendrex slammed his journal shut and tossed it aside. There was no point in dwelling on the past, no use in succumbing to such dark thoughts.

Hendrex dragged himself off the plush jewel-toned meditation pillows in the corner of Zazzie's bedroom and headed for the bathroom. It was already past noon, and he had to report to the Factory to work on Magistrate business, but first, he would go to see Zazzie.

She was precisely what he needed to turn the rough start to his day around. A smile touched his lips as he thought of Zazzie spread naked before him on the bed last night.

There had been a massive storm, and after her feminine rituals, she'd come to him literally soaked from the rain but also between her thighs. Just the memory of his tongue on her honey-coated lips was enough to rush him through his dressing routine.

On his way to Zazzie's office, he stopped to pick up some of her favorite pastries. Mack told him it was what boyfriends were supposed to do, and he hoped it would be a pleasant surprise for Zazzie. He usually never bothered her at work.

The school building was larger than he thought it would be, and somewhat depressing to look at if Hendrex was honest. Even the sparse sprinkling of vegetation around the brick did little to make it look inviting.

He took the steps two at a time, swinging open the double glass paned doors. He stepped into an open hallway and was immediately greeted by the smell. He wasn't entirely sure what the cacophony of smells was, but it wasn't pleasant.

"May I help you?" A tall man came from around the corner.

"Uh, yes, I'm here to see Ms. Monoceros."

"Is she expecting a delivery?"

Hendrex didn't like the man's dismissive tone, but he kept his smile light and shook his head.

"I'm a friend of hers."

Amusement and something malicious danced in the man's eyes.

"She seems to have a lot of friends."

"She is a very social person."

The man shook his head.

"You know what I mean, man, but then again, maybe you don't. Let me make this clear. Zarovia Monoceros is a thot."

"A what?"

"A thot. A dick chaser."

"Excuse me?" Hendrex set the pastries on the empty receptionist's desk and got in the man's face.

The man chuckled and patted Hendrex on the shoulder before taking a step back.

"Hey, man. I'm just trying to help you out here. Zarovia obviously has you sprung. I've been there, but don't get your hopes up. You're just the flavor of the month."

The receptionist emerged from the door behind her desk. If she hadn't, Hendrex would have torn into the man.

"Sorry, have you been waiting long?"

Hendrex turned to the young girl at the desk, and the man left without another word through the front door.

"No, I am looking for Zarovia Monoceros," he said in as calm of a voice as he could manage.

The woman smiled.

"Oh! She gets a lot of deliveries from admirers. I can take this to her, so you can get back to your route."

The girl's statement only further fueled his anger. What kind of place did Zazzie work that her coworkers spoke so freely about her private life? Was she really that popular with men? Did Hendrex really look like a delivery person?

"I'm a friend of Zarovia's, and I don't think she would appreciate a coworker telling her business to a stranger."

The girl flushed bright red and immediately reached for the phone on her desk.

"I am so sorry. Let me see if Ms. Monoceros is busy. I will call her myself."

***

When her phone rang, the last thing she expected was for it to be Hendrex. He never bothered her at work. She quickly organized the papers on her desk and made sure her clothes and hair were in order before going to the lobby area to meet with him.

"Hendrex! What a surprise," she gushed, genuinely excited for him to be there.

He smiled at her, but it didn't reach his eyes. Even as they embraced, the warmth she usually felt in his arms wasn't there.

"I know you're busy, but I thought I'd bring you a snack," he said and practically shoved a pastry box into her hands.

He turned and was out of the door before Zarovia even had a chance to ponder his shitty attitude.

She tossed the pastries on the receptionist's desk and went after him. Why would he come all the way to her job to be a dick to her?

She caught up to him at the public transit stop on the corner.

"What the hell, Hendrex?"

"I should be asking you the same thing!"

Zazzie let go of him and crossed her arms over her chest.

"I'm at fucking work. I don't have time to be sitting out here arguing with you. Spit it out, Hendrex Andromeda. What bug crawled up your ass since last night?"

"Ask your trash-ass coworkers. I've got to get to the Factory."

The public transit arrived, and Hendrex got on without another word. Frustrated, Zazzie returned to the building. Heather, the front desk girl, looked suspiciously busy and red in the face.

"Heather, did you say anything to offend my friend?"

Heather stopped what she was doing and looked up sheepishly.

"I'm sorry, Ms. Monoceros. I thought he was a delivery guy. You're always getting flowers and stuff delivered, and I may have implied that you were popular with men. I said that I could finish the delivery for him if he had other deliveries," the young women rushed out.

Zazzie bit her lip to keep from cursing.

"Anything else?"

"Well, he was chatting with Mr. Laughton before while I was in the restroom, and I may have overheard a few things," she said.

"Like what?"

"Mr. Laughton called you a thot and warned your friend not to get attached."

"Motherfucker," Zazzie cursed, forgetting in her anger that she was at work.

"Heather, please stay out of my personal affairs from

now on. Also, is Peggy from HR available?”

“I promise never to make a mistake like this again. Please don’t report me to HR. I need this job. My boyfriend just got laid off, and…” Zazzie held up her hand to stop Heather’s little sob story.

“You overstepped, do it again, and I will surely go to HR about it, but this time you’re off the hook. Now, is anyone in HR here or not?”

“Yes, they had a luncheon today, so everyone should be in their office.”

“Great,” Zazzie said and marched off to HR.

She may be willing to give Heather a pass this time, but Derrick had a whole other thing coming. Once she had that handled, she could figure out what to do about Hendrex. She couldn’t be sure if he was pissed about Derrick or pissed that he’d been mistaken for a delivery man. It wasn’t that Hendrex hadn’t known about her sexually free lifestyle. They’d discussed it before, and while he wasn’t a fan of it, he hadn’t condemned her or treated her any differently because of it. Granted, knowing and meeting one of her past partners were entirely different.

No, for Hendrex, it was being mistaken for the delivery man that would have been a massive hit to his ego. He hadn’t said much about it, but it was clear he struggled with not being part of the Ruling Council and living off of her while he got on his feet. Either was a major setback in their undefined relationship.

Campaign

Jasmine Hyperion sat in front of what used to be the gate to her home. The place had been technically off-limits since the fall. Now more of a sacred memorial than a through traffic zone. She sat amongst the flowers left in honor of the dead. She'd lit a few of the candles that still had wick enough to light and wax enough to burn.

As a new Ruling Council member, she didn't have to worry about anyone questioning her penchant for spending so much time there. She picked up a discarded bit of ash and drew the sacred symbols. She knew Ceres was gone, but she couldn't help the impulse. Couldn't help but desire to see if things weren't as dire as they had seemed that dreadful night. That instead of nothing, instead of a cosmic void, Ceres had somehow survived. That one day, those survivors would deem it safe enough to re-open the gate and welcome back those who fled without malice or distrust.

It was wishful thinking, at best. The Runes didn't glow or hum as they should. Instead, they lay upon the brick as lifeless as those who died in its shadow. Jasmine swiped away the ash, a lone tear escaping her eye before she turned away and headed back inside.

She needed to prep for the Council meeting that

evening, and she still had Aura history papers to review. The Factory inside was noisy, not from the machinery but from the families currently in residence. It was a shame to see her people crammed in every nook and cranny. There was no privacy for anyone. The families even shared a communal bathroom. It was nothing like the abundance Ceres had offered them and they were accustomed to. Jasmine crossed through the sleeping quarters, nodding to parents and reminding children of their class schedule.

I will get my people back to safety.

She chanted the mantra to herself as she made her way to her designated office. She was too busy chanting to notice her path being blocked. She slammed head-first into Hendrex Andromeda. His thick arms encircled her waist and held her at an odd angle in mid-air.

"Careful there, Ruling Two."

His baritone washed over her body, sending waves of arousal to her core. She cleared her throat and straightened her clothes after he set her upright.

"Please, call me Jasmine." Her voice came out breathy and unsure.

Hendrex smiled down at her, radiant white teeth framed by full lips and stubble darkening his sharp jaw. Jasmine bit her lip. She missed his cleanly shaven face but wouldn't mind the roughness of his fresh look against her skin if he dared to ever kiss her—yet another example of wishful thinking on her part. Hendrex Andromeda only knew she existed because she had been elected to the Ruling Council. He'd seemed so untouchable back in Ceres. She'd only ever lusted for him from afar.

"No can do, Ruling Two. Rules are rules, and I know how much you love following the rules."

Jasmine wasn't sure if his words were a slight or an observation. Either way, she was once again behind the curve. Hendrex had already pivoted away from her and proceeded down the hall toward the Magistrate's office.

***

The sun's rays felt like sandpaper to her tear-swollen eyes, even being late in the day. Still, Carrie refused to wear the large bug-eyed sunglasses as she laid what was left of her father to rest in the family plot. His grave marker would hold no date, just his name, Maximus. He might not have been the best father in the world, but he'd cared for her deeply. So, like the dutiful daughter she was, she stood by his side, even in death. Accepting the condolences of people who were angrier at the perceived loss of control in Langsmith than the loss of Maximus himself.

The Council hadn't even waited until his burial before requesting an audience with her. That whole fiasco meant Carrie was forced to endure this alone. Having Greg present now wasn't in either of their best interests. That didn't mean Carrie didn't wish he were present. She needed his strength. With the ceremony over, the crowd had thinned enough to justify Carrie leaving. Still, before she could head for her waiting car, Brody appeared by her side.

He cleared his throat and bowed.

"I am truly sorry for your loss."

Carrie clenched her hands into fists. Her nails bit into her skin, the pain a reminder that she couldn't slap the shit out of Brody, despite everything he had done for her and hadn't done for her father. Even if she couldn't be physically violent with the man, that didn't mean she couldn't show her distaste otherwise. Besides, Brody had already expressed his condolences before the ceremony. This was too much, even for his usual boot-licking tendencies.

"What the fuck do you want?"

Brody straightened; his thin lips pressed together in a manner that made his entire mouth disappear.

"I am here on behalf of the Royal family. They wish an audience with you."

Carrie scowled. After the Council members, the last thing she wanted to do was deal with her distant relatives. They were worse than anyone Carrie had ever met; even Maura was a doll in comparison. Still, she could hardly turn down a summons from them. With a sigh, she let Brody escort her to her car and let the driver know the change of plans. Thankfully, Brody didn't attempt to slide into the backseat with her.

If there was one boon from this, it was that it seemed Brody had set his eyes on a different avenue for increasing his stature in Vampire society. Carrie pulled out her phone and dialed Greg's number. He wouldn't join her on this excursion either, but he needed to know she would be out of town for a while. The Royal family would never set foot in Langsmith. Not to mention, they would never go to her, even in this time of distress.

Greg answered his phone immediately, but judging by the noise in the background, he wasn't alone.

"Give me a moment," Greg said.

She didn't have to wait long.

"Are you on your way home?" he asked.

"No, actually, I'm headed out of town."

"Did something happen? Where should I meet you?"

Carrie smiled. His concern always gave her butterflies.

"I'm fine. I just have some family business to attend to that requires a solo trip."

"Are you sure that's a good idea right now?"

"No, but I can't stay, and you can't come along. I promise I will keep in touch."

There was a long pause before he exhaled heavily.

"Okay, but if at any moment you feel you need me..."

Carrie swallowed hard. She needed him now, but she couldn't say that. Their relationship was complicated, to say the least. Their current arrangement was all she had to offer him, especially in all the turmoil.

"I'll call, I promise."

Carrie hung up before her heart spoke. She pulled her sweater tighter over her chest. Carrie had a feeling nothing good would come from her visit. All she could hope for was that she would be allowed to leave and return to her normal life once it was over. There was no telling what might happen once she set foot on the Royal compound. Even her father had kept her far away from the place.

She knew enough about her Royal relatives to know that bringing one of Maura's Men amongst them was basically a death sentence for Greg. She should have been more concerned with that fact from the beginning.

How was he supposed to fit into her life now? Did it really matter that much?

There were so many questions that Carrie didn't have the answers to. So many questions she could have and should have asked before today. Either way, she was going to find them out. If the Royal family was trafficking Aura, Carrie would be able to tell. She knew the difference now. Could sense it now that all Aura blood had dissipated from her system. There was an extra something that those who consumed Aura blood gave off. It was hard to describe. It wasn't quite charisma, but the people seemed less death-like.

Granted, her only experience with this was from turned Vampires. Born Vampires weren't dead, and so the darkness wasn't as strong in them in that way. Their darkness sprang from a source quite different. A source lauded almost like a myth.

Carrie wouldn't be a victim to the whims of her family any longer. She would gather the information she needed and use it to help broker peace in Langsmith. It was the least she could do after all the destruction and chaos her father had caused.

***

Zazzie hung her bag on one of the decorative hooks on the wall. The smell of sauteed vegetables wafted from the kitchen. The clank and sizzle drew her to the room used mainly to create herbal remedies and skin care for her shop. Hendrex bustled around the kitchen. She stood in the doorway a little longer, admiring how his muscles rippled in his black tee.

If it weren't for the tense set of his jaw and the angry way he tossed the spinach and garlic in the pan, she might have stripped right then and there and made herself the main course for the evening.

"You're home late," Hendrex said, sliding the vibrant green spinach onto a plate next to a perfectly roasted piece of chicken.

Hendrex had taken to cooking technologies better than most of the men from Ceres. Zarovia, while mostly vegetarian, wasn't going to complain when a man wanted to cook for her instead of forcing the gender roles to be a women's place.

"I stopped by the Factory to check in with the kids there and drop off a second proposal to the Ruling Council about finding space to hold classes. I guess we just missed each other."

"I guess," he muttered.

"My proposal has been tabled, I'm sure you already knew that, but that isn't going to deter me. The school we discussed officially has its first students."

Hendrex looked up in surprise, and Zazzie smiled. Maybe he wasn't that upset.

"Who?"

He filled a glass of wine for her and a glass of water for himself before bringing them over to the linen-draped table in the corner of her small kitchen. Zazzie moved to sit at the table. Hendrex held the chair out for her and even draped a cloth napkin across her lap.

"Daphne Orion and Sarah Greywulf."

He'd gone all out this evening, and that only made Zazzie feel worse. Was he trying to overcompensate for some feeling of inadequacy? Was he showing her just how good she had it with him before dropping her ass like she dropped Darnell earlier?

"Sarah Greywulf?" Hendrex raised an eyebrow before lighting a candle between them and taking a seat.

"Yes, she helped Daphne in a situation, and I think it would be good for both girls to form a friendship while they help each other adjust to the new way of things."

She kept the conversation light but knew that eventually, the other shoe would drop. Hendrex bowed his head, his lips moving silently in prayer before he began to eat.

"I thought the school would be focused on Aura children. I've dealt with the people enough to know they won't feel comfortable with their children practicing energies among strangers. Especially with everything that has happened with The Resistance."

Zazzie shook her head and thanked the ancestors for providing the bounty before them.

"I'm not going to deny other supernatural children the opportunity to learn about our people. If anything, it will only foster a better sense of community. The more we understand about each other, the greater the opportunity and probability of coexisting peacefully."

Hendrex's shoulders were tense as he unnecessarily sawed into the perfectly tender chicken on his plate. They ate in silence for a while before Hendrex spoke again.

"I'm sorry. I didn't mean to negate your good news. I am happy there is progress being made in that regard."

He reached across the table and took her hand in his. He brought her hand to his lips and pressed a kiss to her open palm.

"I know you are just voicing the concerns you have. I know you care about this as much as I do. It sucks that this will be an uphill battle, but I am prepared to fight for it."

"As am I, but don't you think maybe starting out with just the Aura until things are more settled might make the transition easier?"

"There is nothing easy about change. The children are more open to this than their parents."

"Of course, but their parents are who you need to convince. There are already those who refuse to send their children to the human schools."

Zazzie rolled her eyes.

"I know, which is unfortunate, but that is their right as parents to decide. I don't expect to win everyone over. I just want there to be space for those who are willing to open up and try things differently."

Hendrex pressed another kiss across her knuckles before letting her hand go.

"Lucky for you, you seem to be quite popular."

The warm feeling of his kisses on her hand cooled instantly.

"What is that supposed to mean?"

"Nothing, Zarovia. I had a fairly uneventful day. More of the same uncertainty. At least, I already have an established identity, so I am a little ahead of others."

Zazzie wasn't quite ready to change the subject, but

she also didn't want to argue with him over dinner.

"Did you look for jobs again? I told you it's fine that you focus on helping others right now."

Hendrex set his fork down.

"No, it isn't fine. I can't be the man I want to be for you if I don't have a thing to offer you besides physical intimacy."

Zazzie smirked.

"Please! I rather enjoy physical intimacy with you. If you hadn't noticed last night, I could give you a refresher."

Hendrex smiled, but it didn't quite reach his eyes. "Physical intimacy comes easy for you."

"Does this have anything to do with what happened at my job?"

"Not at all!"

"Then, what?"

"I told you already. I want to be a man worthy of you," Hendrex said.

The pain in his voice was almost her undoing. His sense of responsibility had always weighed Hendrex down. It was one of the things that had kept them apart for so long. His sense of duty, devotion to family, and loyalty to the Aura were all things she loved about him. Yet, they were also the things that seemed to always get in the way of their happiness together.

Maybe she was selfish, but she liked Hendrex in this domestic role, his focus almost solely on her. It would not last, it couldn't, but she was going to enjoy every minute of it while she still could. Zazzie reached for her wine glass and took a sip. Hendrex kept his head down as he ate.

"Not worthy? Is that what all this was supposed to prove?" Zazzie waved to the romantic spread before them, "I don't need any of this, Hendrex. I just want you. Can't that be enough? Can't just being with me be enough for you?"

Hendrex didn't say anything.

"Asshole." Zazzie stood and started to undress. Not for him, but because she was too angry for the amount of clothing she still had on.

Zazzie unraveled her locs from the top of her head, letting them fall loosely over her shoulders. Next, she pulled her shirt off and let it fall to the floor before reaching behind her back to unhook her bra. Zazzie was not a fan of such arcane bindings, but they were required for her work. Usually, she took it off as soon as she entered the door, but she had been too excited to tell Hendrex her news.

Hendrex looked up from his plate, the heat of his gaze warming the skin of her exposed breasts, her nipples puckering under his scrutiny, but he was out of luck tonight. She was too pissed to allow him the satisfaction of her body. But that didn't mean she wouldn't enjoy the look on his face as she pleasured herself in front of him. She walked to the kitchen and propped herself up on the counter. She spread her legs wide so he could see everything she was doing to herself.

"Touch yourself," he demanded.

A thrill ran through her body.

"Be more specific."

Hendrex set down his fork and crossed his arms over his chest.

"Hands on your breasts, knead them like the dough for the bread we baked this last weekend."

Zazzie complied with his wishes, cupping and squeezing the soft flesh. Hendrex watched intently, his mouth slightly open as his breathing went shallow with arousal.

"Pinch your nipples. Gently."

Zazzie pinched them just enough to feel the pressure on the sensitive nubs. Electricity shot from her nipples and down to her core. Her womb contracted, pulsating in anticipation. His tongue slid out to lick his thick lips, and he adjusted himself in his chair.

"Now stop and come eat your food before it gets cold," he said and turned his attention back to his plate.

Zazzie let out a frustrated sigh. Hendrex knew Zazzie preferred instant gratification when it came to sex. Yes, she could wait for a bit, but she wasn't one to deny her body what it craved. Yet, here he was being stubborn with their play, which only pissed her off further.

"Don't be sad, love, I just want you well-fed before I feast on you."

"Oh, really?"

She tried not to let the disappointment show in her voice. Zazzie had no intention of letting him touch her tonight, but he was still trying to be stingy with the dick when she was obviously pissed at him. Could he be any more infuriating?

Hendrex didn't answer, just went back to eating. Zazzie was done. She slid off the counter and strode into her bedroom.

***

A true goddess lay before him. His Zarovia. She rested so peacefully, the steady rise and fall of her bare breasts a fascinating temptation. He wanted this forever. He needed to make this a forever thing. Only, there were things he needed to do for himself before he could truly make her his.

He pressed a soft kiss to her temple and moved to cradle her in his arms. He had fucked up Royally last night. Yes, he'd been pissed about her coworkers. What they had said about her was unprofessional and concerning. But what had bothered him the most was her inability to see from his side of things. She might be okay with him living off of her, but he wasn't. He'd prided himself on his independence his entire adult life and his status amongst his people. Now, he had neither.

How could he possibly offer her a future when he had no actual future to offer her? Not to mention, they hadn't exactly qualified what this was between them. Hendrex was absolutely clear that Zarovia was his past, present, and future, but that didn't mean she felt the same. She always introduced him as a friend, or worse, a friend she was helping for a while. How could she not see how that was unacceptable to him?

Then there was the issue of the physical intimacy between them. Zazzie had never denied him access to her body until last night. Hell, last night had been the first time since the fall of Ceres that they'd gone to bed separately, that he hadn't spent hours pleasuring her until Zazzie begged and pleaded to feel him inside of her. Of course, Hendrex always held off on that as much as they both craved it. He wanted there to be something special for them on their Binding night.

It wasn't that they had never done so before. There had been one slip up that Hendrex would never regret, but he was a man of principle. He could wait for another taste of true heaven. A chance to be with Zazzie without the barrier of modern latex. Without the uncertainty that plagued them now.

He would wait until Zazzie was entirely his before fully enjoying the holy communion of their flesh. Zazzie whimpered and snuggled closer. Her skin had cooled to the touch, and he reluctantly pulled the covers over her body, obscuring his view.

In the morning, they would have breakfast before she left for work. Hendrex would make sure of it. He needed to step up his game to spend time with her, and not in bed. With Zazzie's work schedule and his responsibilities as Magistrate, there were plenty of missed opportunities for both of them throughout the week. He would have joy in the morning before the fear and uncertainty took over. He would make things right with Zazzie before she had to face the very people who spoke so poorly of her to him. It was the least he could do.

As soon as his day started in earnest, Hendrex would check in with the others. Donovan, Mack, Tyr, and the Vampires dubbed Maura's Men were set to meet and discuss a plan of action to maintain the peace in Langsmith. There was so much to discuss, so many variables and decisions to make. Hendrex thought being removed from the Ruling Council would finally free him of his sense of duty to the Aura. It had not. Instead, it only cemented it in his mind.

Hendrex knew he had to make Zazzie's school a reality. He wanted that for her and for their people. Yet, there was so much else that needed to be accomplished before that could safely be a reality. He didn't want to discourage Zarovia from her dream, but he would have to find a way to stall her. Especially with the lack of structure surrounding the acclimation of the Aura to their new world. Relations with other Supernaturals were still tense. Although, chains of communication between involved groups were open and some alliances formed, the people as a whole hadn't accepted those alliances. Zarovia wanted an open school for all. That would be a hard sell right now. He would hate to see her fail because of other people's prejudice.

Going through his checklist for the following day, Hendrex made a mental note to discuss the school's situation with Tyr. He had to see that while Sarah was a trustworthy ally to the Aura, having her involved with the school put both groups in a bad position. Especially after the fall of Ceres and the Vampire threat. Tensions were too high.

Hendrex closed his eyes, but his mind still ran full speed ahead. He knew he could always wake Zazzie and distract himself with her pleasure, but she needed her rest. Zazzie never talked about being tired, but how could she not be with everything she had on her plate. Working with the children in human schools during the week, running her metaphysical shop during the weekends, and of course, engaging in sexual activities with him most nights. He should have felt bad about the latter, but he couldn't bring himself to. The last week had been hard on all of them, and any happiness they could get a hold of was something to protect and cherish.

Breaking Ground

A chill washed over Carrie as soon as she crossed into the city limits of Oracle. The town was the home of the Vampire elite. Unassuming as it was, Carrie felt this place was much more dangerous than Langsmith, even if it didn't hold the same magical feel.

The town itself wasn't so bad. It was the massive estates that housed Carrie's Royal relatives that really gave her the creeps. They were real-life monsters. Scarier than the bogeyman, more vicious than any serial killer, and more conniving than the worst of politicians.

In their presence, the wrong word or even a tilt of the head could mean instant death or imprisonment. Another reason her father had shielded her from them as best he could. He relished their attention and was more like them than Carrie had ever imagined. Still, somehow, he'd known they could not be trusted in her presence, and now, here she was, walking right into the lion's den with the last Vampire she would ever trust, Brody.

The car pulled up to the main house, and Brody climbed out and offered her his hand. She ignored it and helped herself out of the vehicle.

Brody rolled his eyes. "I know I'm not your favorite person, and frankly, you aren't mine either, but if we both want to be able to leave here at some point, we will need to trust each other just this once.”

Carrie shook her head.

“I’ll never trust you.”

“Suit yourself, but don’t say I didn’t try to warn you. Your father did you a disservice keeping you naïve to the truth of things.”

“On that, we can agree,” Carrie said before marching up the stone steps to the door.

The massive glass and wrought iron doors swung open, and a servant bowed and gestured for her to come in. Just like its inhabitants, the manor was ostentatious and pretentious. Gold and Carrera marble blinded you with dizzying light and spirals.

The servant led Brody and Carrie to the parlor. A massive fireplace roared with bright red flames, framed by large floor-to-ceiling bookcases. The heat from the flames provided an almost stifling heat to the already stuffy and uncomfortable atmosphere.

“Master will be with you shortly,” the servant said before closing the double doors and retreating.

Carrie didn’t dare sit down. She didn’t want to be seen as getting comfortable in this space. She remembered the last time she had come here. It had been for a party. She’d been kept to the corner of the room with the other females, heavily guarded and yet propped up in grand seats like dolls on display for the droves of men present.

Brody didn’t have the same hang-ups as she did. He waltzed to one of the overstuffed leather chairs and settled in as if it were his own private study.

“You should get comfortable. I doubt we will be leaving here anytime soon. Master Merwin has a tendency to keep people waiting.”

Carrie snorted.

“Only those he deems unimportant. I am a female

relative. He'll be here soon."

As if her words conjured him, Merwin swept into the room.

"Sorry to keep you waiting, my dear. I wish I had been able to attend the burial, but there was a pressing family issue here."

Merwin swept Carrie into a hug before she could protest. Vampires weren't very sentimental. This show of affection was above and beyond, even for the newest turned Vampires, let alone a member of the aristocracy.

Family or not, the situation unnerved Carrie. That he would feel so cavalier as to touch her, let alone hug her.

"There was nothing to bury. It was all for show. No need to feel sentimental," Carrie said.

Merwin pulled away and smiled.

"I see you aren't as humanized as I was led to believe. That's a relief."

"There are many rumors about me. The only truth to them is that I don't plan to suffer fools after me for some perceived gain in status."

Merwin walked to a decanter of what was no doubt some obscenely expensive dark liquor and poured two glasses. He offered her one, and she accepted it. Carrie wasn't much of a drinker, but she didn't want to decline his offer of the drink. It would show weakness not to accept. If she didn't trust herself to drink around him, then it would show she wasn't as confident and set in her ways as she just said.

"Thank you." Carrie took a sip of the brown liquid; it went down smooth before filling her belly with a pleasant warmth.

Merwin took a sip of his as well, his eyes studying her over the rim of his glass.

"What are we to do with you, Caroline? We cannot let someone as precious to this family as you are run loose with hooligans. Especially those involved with your own father's death. How would that look?"

Carrie set her glass down on a coaster and smiled.

"I will adhere to the traditions and grieve for the required time. I have a safe place to do so. As far as who I associate with, that is none of your concern. I am but a distant relative. My standing isn't as high as you or others like to think. Those hooligans, as you call them, were acting in self-defense. I am not naïve enough to not realize what a monster my father had become. His misdeeds warranted retaliation but not murder. I promise you the one who murdered my father is no friend of mine."

Merwin raised an eyebrow at her.

"And what do you know of these supposed misdeeds of your fathers?"

So, this is why he wanted to see me so soon?

Carrie looked over at Brody. He stared at the opposite wall as if he wasn't hanging on their every word. Brody knew everything. If he was working with Merwin, then Merwin must be in on it too. Carrie turned back to her relative. She studied him. She didn't sense any Aura blood on him, but there was something else there that she couldn't quite place. Carrie knew well that there was something about the Royal family that set them apart from everyone else.

There were rumors of aliens or mystical powers beyond even what the Aura had. Yet, she had witnessed nothing out of the ordinary in her limited interactions with her family.

"He was trafficking blood slaves. I know it's posh for born Vamps to drink from live sources, but to force people against their will is unseemly, especially when there are those willing," Carrie said.

Merwin's smile widened. It seemed she'd said

precisely what he had hoped to hear from her. That she was unaware of the connection to the Aura. Her playing naïve was the best for this situation. She wasn't sure how Merwin would react if she told him everything. She also wasn't sure Merwin was aware of her father's source of Aura. If Langsmith was already known as an Aura hot spot or not. Merwin wasn't likely to share such information with a female. If Carrie told him everything, about the Aura, about Maura's Men, about Molly? She didn't want to think of what that could mean. Merwin was her only chance of convincing the Council to forgo attacking the other supernatural in Langsmith. Granted, most of the drama was between Rogue factions and the Aura.

"Don't worry your pretty little head about those things. I'm sure your father had his reasons. There may be willing participants, but not all willing can be trusted or have the right genetic makeup to sustain us at our peak."

Just nod and agree, Carrie. If he thinks you will just go on quietly without raising a fuss, maybe we can get out of here sooner.

"I'm sorry, should I not worry about the reputation of the family? We represent the honor and future of our species. If we allow ourselves to be swayed by greed, how can we claim to be better than the Rogues that threaten to expose us at every turn?"

Merwin's smile faded, and he slammed down his glass.

"How dare you compare our great line to such animals?"

"How dare you ask me to ignore atrocious acts that make us no better than animals."

Merwin raised a hand as if to strike Carrie, but she didn't flinch. She couldn't be silent in the face of such atrocity. She couldn't stand by and continue to let innocents be stolen and mistreated.

"You would strike me for telling the truth?"

"You have no idea what the truth is, little girl," Merwin spat, lowering his hand.

"And yet, I doubt you will enlighten me to what is actually going on."

"It's not a matter for you. Your focus should be on finding a suitable mate to continue the line, not meddle in affairs beyond your intellect."

Carrie picked up her glass and downed the rest of the alcohol before setting it down and signaling for Brody to get up.

"I appreciate your condolences, but I shall take my leave. My lack of intellect is tired of trying to wrap itself around your misogynist bullshit."

Merwin gasped, stunned by her words. His shock gave her the perfect opening to exit with her head held high. If only she hadn't run into a massive male chest as she attempted to exit the room. She stumbled back, caught in the male's arms.

"Sorry, miss."

Carrie looked up to see Cain staring down at her. She had met him once or twice in her life. He'd always come across as arrogant and selfish, but now there was an air of defeat about him. Maybe it was the slight bruising visible around his eyes and neck. Someone had really done a number on him.

"No problem. I was just leaving."

She pulled out of his arms and continued her escape from the manor. She could feel the intensity of his gaze on her back. Thankfully, the car that had brought her and Brody still idled out front. She climbed into the back seat and waited a few minutes for Brody, who was a noticeable distance behind her.

"What took you so long?" she snapped.

"Unlike you, I can't just waltz out on a Royal family member. I had to say proper goodbyes."

Carrie glared at him.

"As soon as we are back in Langsmith, don't bother coming to me again, or I will have my guard rip your head from your shoulders."

Brody had the nerve to chuckle.

"I think I am growing to like this side of you."

***

Zazzie awoke completely wrapped around Hendrex's body. She kept her eyes closed, taking a moment to enjoy the feeling of his bare skin against hers. The anger of yesterday could wait. She needed this time of peace with him. It was just their first argument, after all. It was a big one but not something completely insurmountable.

Hendrex shifted, and his large palm cupped the round cheeks of her ass and gave them a squeeze.

"Morning, beautiful."

She opened her eyes slowly, and he was smiling down at her.

"Good morning," she murmured.

He bent his head and pressed a soft kiss to her lips.

"I'm sorry about last night. I was immature and stand-offish. I handled things in the exact opposite fashion of a real man. Please allow me to make it up to you," he said.

Zazzie snuggled closer and dropped soft kisses along his exposed collarbone.

"And just how do you plan to make it up to me?"

Hendrex got out of bed and pulled her out of the warm blankets as well.

"Follow me."

Zarovia followed him to the kitchen. She desperately

hoped it involved more than just a nice chat over breakfast as he went straight to dig something out of the fridge. He produced a bowl of what she knew was homemade chocolate raspberry sauce, her favorite and his. He placed the bowl on the counter before lifting her up next to it. He grabbed the bowl and dove between her thighs.

"Naughty girl, already wet for me," Hendrex groaned. His breath hot on her inner thighs.

"Excuse me, sir, but I am always wet when you are around."

He chuckled, and she felt the cool stickiness of the sauce on her as he coated her with his fingers. The difference in temperature on her heated flesh had her gripping the counter. Hendrex's hot mouth followed soon after.

"Fuck!"

He latched onto her clit and suckled the sauce from her lower lips. When it was mostly gone, Hendrex reapplied it. The alternating sensation of his cool finger strokes followed by his hot tongue and powerful suction quickly sent her over the edge. Hendrex gripped her hips, delving his tongue into her as her first orgasm racked her. Her greedy inner muscles clenched tightly as if to draw him further and deeper inside. He hummed low in his throat.

The vibration heightened the electricity that danced through her nervous system. As her climax subsided, Hendrex removed his tongue and replaced it with two thick fingers. Hendrex surged up her body and kissed her. The salty-sweet taste of her arousal mixed with her favorite dessert topping was almost enough to send her back over the edge. Hendrex intuitively seemed to know that and curled his fingers until they pressed right against her g-spot.

"Come again," he said, nipping her lip with his teeth.

Zazzie threw her head back and moaned as another orgasm tore through her body. Hendrex licked and teased her exposed nipples with his tongue while he eased his thick fingers in and out of her body until she was a shuddering mess sprawled before him on her kitchen counter.

This is what she needed from Hendrex. Not a man to take care of her or pay her bills. She appreciated that, but it wasn't necessary. What she needed from him was his undivided attention. She needed him, plain and simple, and she wanted the D like crazy. Being together was what they both had waited years for, and as much as she loved what she had with him now, she wanted more, so much more.

***

Hendrex shut off the hot water and grabbed the fluffy lavender towel from the rack beside the shower-tub combo. He quickly toweled off his body. The soft terry fibers felt weird against his newly shaved head. Zazzie had balked at the idea of him losing his locs, but she'd agreed to help him with the task after he explained he wanted to start fresh. Not just with her, but with his life.

He gingerly stepped out of the tub and onto the colorful woven mat, careful not to slip on the glossy white tile, and wrapped the towel around his waist. It gaped with every step he took out to the plush jewel-toned bedroom, creating a breeze against his inner thighs.

They stung a little from the tiny scratches and crescent puncture from Zazzie's nails and love bites. A smile brightened his face just thinking of the time they'd spent together that morning. They may have gone to bed in a bad space, but if anything, the experience only cemented for Hendrex that Zazzie was the one, his one.

They had great conversations, shared the same taste in food and music, not to mention the fireworks in bed.

Hendrex dug into the black duffel his twin brother, Maclovis, had given him with clothes to tide him over as he transitioned into life in the human world. The black bag a stunning void against Zazzie's busy printed bedding. Inside the bag was no better. There was nothing but a sea of black and denim to be found, no matter how many times he looked or wished differently. The laid-back bouncer look was Mack's style, not his. As soon as he sorted out his job situation, he would first, get clothing that better suited his taste and second, ask Zazzie to Bind with him.

He pulled on a black shirt that felt two sizes too small and pants that felt three sizes two big. At least Mack had included a thick leather belt so Hendrex wouldn't have to endure the loose-fitting style humans called 'sagging.' Fully dressed, he made his way through the eclectic rainbow of Zazzie's home to the kitchen. Zazzie had left for the day shortly after her fifth orgasm at his hand. She was usually gone before he woke, needing to get to her office well before the school day started.

It was one of the reasons the weekends were his favorite time. But he might just force himself to get up sooner during the week since it meant waking up to Zazzie. Buried in the million and one pillows and snuggling deep in his embrace. At least, until her side business opened in the early afternoon. The one area of her space he didn't venture into. He couldn't say he cared for her exploitation of her energy for monetary gain, but that was something they could discuss when he could offer her an alternative. For now, he fixed himself a bowl of granola and oat milk before checking the new smartphone Mack had acquired for him.

Hendrex wasn't completely unused to human

technology, but he had underestimated just how much technological advancement had changed how things were done in the last ten years. Texting was preferred over actual calls. One could now do almost anything from handheld devices. A picture of Mack lit up Hendrex's phone. Mack was twisting his face into different silly positions as a tiny camera jumped at the bottom of the screen. Hendrex had learned this was called picture time or something along those lines. Mack had something against the company that made that kind of phone, so instead, the app was called something about hanging.

None of it made sense to Hendrex, but the ease of the technology was growing on him.

"Good morning, brother."

"What the hell did you do to your head?"

"I needed a change," Hendrex said before shoving a bite of cereal into his mouth.

"You still eating that vegetarian nonsense?"

Hendrex crunched it loudly with an open mouth as he spoke, "Don't knock it 'til you try it."

"Yeah, I'd rather not knock out my teeth," Mack snorted.

Hendrex swallowed his food and wiped his mouth. "I take it you have a reason for calling since we planned to meet in less than an hour?"

Mack's face remained neutral.

"Can't I just call my twin brother to say what's up?"

"No," Hendrex laughed.

"Alright, fine. I wanted to run some news by you before the meeting."

"Alright, shoot."

"There are rumors about the Vampire response to what happened."

Hendrex sat up.

"Okay, we knew it would come sooner rather than

later. Is the Vampire Council willing to talk?”

“I plan to have a chat with Xander and the others about that,” Mack said.

“So, what exactly are you running by me, brother?”

None of what Mack said was too surprising or anything that couldn’t have been left to be said later during the meeting.

“I know things are a little convoluted now that there is a new Ruling Council, but I could really use your advice on how to approach this with them.”

Hendrex sighed. He may not be on the Ruling Council any longer, but he may as well be with how many people still came to him with Council business.

“You should technically bring this to them, but as part of the Super Team, I guess I can provide some guidance.”

“X-Men.”

“Whatever!”

“Look, it’s not looking good for us as far as finding a peaceful solution. Maybe if one of their precious born Vamps hadn’t been killed…”

Hendrex shook his head.

“Well, we can’t change that now, can we?”

Mack’s eyes darted around him as if he was unsure if he should continue.

“Maybe?”

Hendrex glared at his brother. He had no idea what kind of dark things Mack had come across in his time away from the fold, but if he was suggesting reanimating Maximus somehow, that was far darker magic than anyone should ever play with. Hendrex decided it best to play dumb.

“What do you mean, maybe?”

“Well, there may be one way, but the person who would need to do it was one of the people in on the killing, so it's the longest of long shots," Mack said.

"You aren't making any sense, and I'm sure I don't want to know what you know to make what you said make sense."

"Right, even if it could happen, resurrecting that asshole wouldn't be good for anyone."

A notification slid across the top of the screen, partially cutting off Hendrex's view of his twin. It was time he headed to the Shifter Compound.

"Listen, we should discuss this more at the meeting. I'll see you in a bit."

Hendrex hung up before Mack could drag out the conversation. Shoving one last bite into his mouth, Hendrex deposited his bowl into the black granite sink and winced as his spoon clanked around the delicate porcelain bowl. There would be hell to pay if he cracked Zazzie's antique dishes, but he didn't have time to check for damage.

His schedule was precisely timed, and any delay would throw off his entire day. Keeping up with routine had helped with his adjustment to his new life. He was no longer part of the Ruling Council. He could no longer call Ceres his home. He was in the middle of a personal and societal crisis, and still, he refused to give up the illusion of having everything together. With everything that had happened in the last couple of months, he needed that last shred of his dignity to cling to.

✳✳✳

Zarovia sat across from Sarah and Daphne's guardians. The air was thick with tension. It crackled like static as the Alpha energy exuding from Sequoia Greywulf collided with that of the young Sarah Greywulf. Zarovia could only imagine their household being like walking on eggshells. So much energy bouncing against each other was bound to cause an explosion every now and again.

Sarah sat in the corner opposite Daphne, arms crossed over her chest. She stared at the ceiling and refused to look at anyone. Daphne, on the other hand, had shrunken into herself and stared at the ground. Her anger and confidence quickly turned to a droll submission the second her mother walked through the door.

"So, what's the plan here? Is Sarah suspended for fighting?" Sequoia's concern was clear in her eyes.

"The fight wasn't technically on school grounds, and given the situation, taking either girl out of school would only exacerbate the problem. What I am suggesting is that you allow me to work with the girls after school," Zarovia said.

She had to tread lightly with her words here. Although there was no doubt Sequoia Greywulf knew about the Aura, she needed to maintain Sarah's trust if her plan was going to work. In the same vein, Daphne's mother wouldn't be comfortable discussing Aura energies in front of a stranger.

Daphne's mother looked at her daughter, a deep sadness in her eyes.

"Whatever you suggest to keep her out of trouble. I would feel better knowing she was under supervised conditions than traipsing around town starting fights," Daphne's mother said.

"I am glad we are all in agreement on this. We shall start next week. I may bring in other instructors and students if warranted."

"Whatever you deem necessary. I will ensure there are no other schedule conflicts with Tyr," Sequoia said.

She didn't wait for Zarovia to reply, just stood and nudged Sarah. The two Shifters left, and the energy in the room fell drastically.

"I appreciate you taking the extra time. I'm just concerned about strangers being involved," Daphne's mother spoke up.

Zarovia sighed.

"The Greywulf's are allies. I can assure you of that, at least. I will also let you know in advance if there are other individuals who are introduced to the class. I want there to be complete transparency and comfort in this situation. It's best for everyone that way."

"I would hope so. Still, I would appreciate more discretion in regard to Daphne's abilities. She has gone through so much already."

"I understand."

Daphne's mother stood then and gathered Daphne before leaving. Zarovia sank back into her chair and took a deep breath. There was plenty of room for error in this situation. She needed a safe space for the girls to learn. They couldn't do it at any of the public schools. There were too many variables to control there. There was the Factory, but with it being the home of so many refugees and the new headquarters, they would be pressed to find the space and privacy to work effectively.

Zarovia pulled out her phone and opened the group chat with her best friends. The last messages were Farrah complaining about her impending Binding ceremony and Enora lamenting pregnancy symptoms. It was a breath of fresh air that her friends seemed intent on focusing on everything but the elephant in the room. She typed in a quick request to meet up after work and shoved her phone back in her pocket.

***

Mack grabbed a chair and sat between Donovan and Tyr. Jaq and Hendrex were sandwiched between Xander and Greg.

"This everybody?" Tyr asked.

"Claude and Shane had things with their mates to attend to," Xander said, and Tyr nodded.

"Alright, so where do we stand with the Vampire Council?"

Xander scowled and turned to Greg, who looked nervous.

"I recently visited the Council with Carrie, and they are more worried about filling the missing space in the Council than worrying about what's happening on the ground here in Langsmith. That may sound like a good thing, but it isn't. With the vacuum of power left by Maximus's murder, there are plenty of Vampires who would love to get revenge on his behalf. Only because avenging his loss is a reason to bolster themselves into his old position," Greg said.

"So, I guess, that means the idea of one of you taking the position is not even an option?" Hendrex asked.

"So far, they haven't directly tied us to his demise, so, I wouldn't say out of the question, just highly unlikely," Xander said.

"What about the Shifters? Are you still able to provide protection for civilians?" Donovan asked Tyr.

Tyr ran a hand over his face.

"I'm getting some serious heat from the Shifter Council about all of this, but for now, yes. As long as my pack is good with the arrangement, I can keep up my end of this bargain. Langsmith is our home too, and as much as we Shifters like to stay out it, this isn't a situation we can Switzerland our way through."

"Thank you. I wish we had anything to report from the Aura delegation. We are overwhelmed with trying to resettle our people, and the Vampire threat is not helping the situation," Jaq said.

"Is that all we have for today?"

Now was the time for Mack to speak.

"Speaking of the Vampire threat. The rumor mills are burning hot with different Rogue leaders dying to get their hands-on Jaq, or any other Aura they happen to encounter. Not just for revenge or a power play, but Maximus wasn't the head of the snake. Whoever was above him in this whole trafficking thing is still out there and willing to pay top dollar for a new supplier."

"Motherfuckers," Jaq cursed.

"We all need to be on alert, limit gatherings, etcetera, until we get a better idea on just who we are dealing with in all of this." Tyr said.

"I agree," Donovan said.

"I'll draft a proposal for a curfew for the Aura," Hendrex said.

Mack could see the strain this whole ordeal was putting on not just his brother but his friends as well. They were all in what seemed to be a no-win situation, but he could only hope they made it out of it mostly unscathed. Since the fall of Ceres, his premonitions had ceased. On the one hand, he'd been glad to have a reprieve. On the other, it worried him. Where were the ancestors in all of this? Had Ceres been the source of that particular aspect of his power? Had the closing of the gate been more than just the end of Ceres, but also the end of his connection to the ancestral plane? There were so many questions and so few answers.

✳✳✳

Jasmine tossed Zarovia Monoceros's proposal on the large table in the center of the conference room.

"Absolutely not. While I very much agree we need a school for our children, Zarovia Monoceros has absolutely zero educational experience to run a school."

"That's not true, and you know it, Ruling Two,"

Disrayan, Ruling One said.

"Zarovia has been working with kids outside of Ceres for years. I think she is perfect for helping our kids transition to this new world," Jaq, Ruling Four said.

Jasmine rolled her eyes. Of course, those two would jump to defend Zarovia. Disrayan was one of Zarovia's best friends. Jaq was the younger brother to Farrah and Bound to Enora, both women close to Zarovia.

She turned to Icarus, who seemed to be more interested in the ceiling than anything of importance. How he had been voted into the Ruling Council was beyond Jasmine, but it wasn't like she could change that now.

"As a counselor, not as an educator."

"I think you're just mad it was Zarovia who pitched this idea. You've been contrary to everything she's touched since primary school," Disrayan scoffed.

Jasmine balled up her fists at her sides, careful to keep them under the table and out of view. She couldn't let them see how upset she was by all of this.

"My personal feelings for Ms. Monoceros aside, she is still completely unqualified for what has been proposed here. Not to mention, her proposed curriculum is anti-Aura tradition and pro blanket assimilation to the human ideal."

Icarus finally dragged his attention from the ceiling and picked up the papers. He studied them carefully before setting them down.

"Honestly, is a school really what we should be talking about right now? What about our people who are bunking up on the Factory floor?"

"Exactly, let's table this school idea and move to more pressing matters."

Disrayan and Jaq exchanged looks before picking up the next proposal in the stack.

"We do have a proposal for incorporating The Resistance with the Security Force," Jaq said.

Another point of contention for Jasmine, but one she was more willing to negotiate on. The Resistance was the reason they were in this mess in the first place. The Resistance was why the Aura had come on the Vampire's radar in the first place, but if the Security Force got involved with them, maybe they could be reformed.

"I don't have a problem with that. The Security Force has dwindled dramatically, and we need protection against the Vampire threat," Jasmine said.

"I'm good with that arrangement as well," Icarus said.

Disrayan nodded at Jaq, and he broke out in a grin that made him almost handsome.

"That settles it then. As Ruling Council, we have ratified our first proposal," he announced.

"Not so fast. We still have to notify and coordinate with Donovan and have the Magistrate write it into the new records."

Jasmine smiled at the mention of the Magistrate. Hendrex Andromeda was the only Andromeda worth a grain of salt.

"I'll inform the Magistrate."

She stood and left the room before anyone could claim the task for themselves.

Jasmine had rare opportunities to be alone with Hendrex, and she wasn't going to miss out on a single one. Maybe this would be when he finally saw her and finally realized they could have a conversation outside of work and the weather.

Before the fall of Ceres, he had been aloof, but she had assumed it was because of his position on the Ruling Council. Now that he had a lesser role, he had more free time. Time she hoped he would choose to spend with her instead of Zarovia Monoceros.

Unfortunately, Hendrex wasn't in his office when she arrived. She let herself be disappointed for a moment before scribbling a note for him to meet with the Council about new business. He stormed into the office, cursing, just as she was leaving.

Jasmine had never seen Hendrex mad before, and if his choice of words wasn't so off-putting, she might have found it sexy.

"Oh, Ruling Two, I apologize for my outburst. I just… never mind. What business did you have with me?"

Jasmine bit her lip as she studied how his tight-fitting clothes hugged the curves and planes of his muscular frame. Belatedly, she realized he had asked her a question.

"Oh, um, we passed our first resolution. If you wouldn't mind coming to the conference room so we could have it written."

Hendrex sighed and nodded. Walking past her to his desk, he opened one of the locked drawers and produce one of the few tomes that had been saved during the fall. The way his thick fingers curved gently around the spine was enough to make Jasmine swoon. She was a sucker for a man who took care of precious belongings. She would give anything to be held so lovingly in his embrace as that book.

Still, his energy seemed off.

"Is there something wrong? I mean, your language earlier and your energy are harsh."

Hendrex looked up and met her gaze. He opened his mouth as if he were about to spill his deepest, darkest secrets only to shake his head.

"It's nothing really, just growing pains with the human world," he said, flashing her a smile that didn't light his face like a real smile would have.

If they were closer, Jasmine would make him tell her the truth, but as their relationship stood, it wasn't her place. Maybe one day, but for now, she smiled and nodded before following him to the conference room where the rest of the Ruling Council and Donovan Mars, the Security Force Commander, waited.

Drunk in Love

They had agreed to meet at Farrah's since it was the closest place with booze. Zarovia didn't bother to knock as she pushed open Farrah's front door. Disrayan and Farrah were already sipping wine and sharing the latest drama in the Aura camp.

"Seriously, you would think that after voting for different leadership, they would understand that things were going to be different!" Disrayan lamented, shaking her head.

Farrah snorted, "Yeah, right. There is a reason they stayed in Ceres so long, even with all the signs that things were going south. The Aura are stuck in their ways. They don't know how to accept change. That was their problem to begin with. You can't expect miracles of them now."

"So, I take it The Resistance being assigned the new Security Force duties didn't go over well?"

Zarovia dropped her bag on the couch and served herself a glass of wine before setting a kettle on the stove for tea. Enora wouldn't be drinking any of the wine, and Zazzie didn't want her to think they didn't think of her condition.

Farrah shook her head and turned off the stove.

"Enora isn't going to make it. She is working late to clear her cases before she has to take leave," Farrah said.

"That girl needs to take a break. I mean, she's going to be dealing with two Andromedas here soon. She's going to need her stamina," Disrayan said.

"I'd take offense, but those Andromeda men are rough," Farrah said.

Zazzie laughed.

"Just the men?"

Farrah scowled at her but said nothing more. Zazzie took that as a sign that Donovan was finally taming Farrah just a bit. The normally say anything, quick-tempered detective had mellowed with her relationship with the Head of the Security Force.

"Speaking of Andromeda men, did you call us here to announce your Binding with Hendrex?" Disrayan asked.

It was Zarovia's turn to scowl.

"That isn't a thing."

Farrah and Disrayan both gave her skeptical looks.

"Girl, who you trying to lie to? Hendrex is basically your house husband right now. When are you going to make an honest man out of him and put a ring on it?" Farrah said.

"Hey! I don't blame you for not wanting to jump the gun on things, but Farrah's right. You are practically Bound already, just without the ceremony," Disrayan said.

"You're one to talk! What about you and Mack?"

Disrayan blushed.

"We decided to forgo the traditional ceremony this time. I wanted to tell you sooner, but things got crazy."

"Are you fucking kidding me?" Enora's outburst from the doorway startled them all.

Farrah cursed and put her gun back in its place under

the counter.

"Girl! You almost got lit up."

Enora rolled her eyes and slammed the door behind her.

"Whatever, your energies must be slipping because I flared three times before coming in."

That was news to them. Enora's flare of energy should have registered with at least one of them.

Farrah saw the others' confusion and shook her head.

"With Donovan here full time, we had to make some adjustments to the apartment."

Zazzie laughed, knowing exactly what adjustments needed to be set up. Donovan was powerful with mind energies, and Farrah had a way of making any sane person lose their cool. With someone with weaker energies, it wasn't a big deal, but for someone like Donovan, a slight slip could invite all sorts of issues.

"Energy dampeners?"

"What else?"

Disrayan moved to turn the water kettle back on.

"Thank you for taking time out of your busy schedule to join us, Doctor."

"Oh, don't start with this whole rest thing again. Need I remind you who barely took time off after being kidnapped by Vampires?"

"I'm not the pregnant one."

"Pregnancy does not make me an invalid."

"No, but you can't blame us for worrying about you. Your job was dangerous before the fall."

"As are all of yours, well, everyone except Zazzie, no offense."

"None taken. I'm not as inclined to violence and turmoil as you three."

Zarovia's friends all laughed at that.

"Maybe not now, but before in training? It's a

wonder how Farrah ended up with the reputation for being reckless when you were most likely to be the instigator," Disrayan said.

Zazzie shrugged.

"People change. This is why both you and Farrah need to cut it out with the gossip. Our people need time to grow. You can't just throw a seed in a field and expect it to immediately sprout. You've got to tend to their needs."

"Speaking of seeds, I heard there was trouble at the school? Is that why you called us here?" Disrayan said.

Zazzie nodded. Not at all surprised that news of a fight involving a Shifter child and an Aura child had made it to the rumor mills, especially since one of them was infamous for being kidnapped and the other was the local Alpha Shifter's daughter.

"Daphne has been targeting fang bangers as a way to process her feelings about what's happened to her."

"That's not good," Enora said.

"No, it isn't. Luckily, Sarah Greywulf stepped in and helped her out this time. I'm having Sarah teach Daphne how to properly defend herself, but with Daphne's increased abilities, I also need a space to help with teaching her how to control them."

"This is bigger than just Daphne. There are so many younger Aura who are showing increased abilities since the surge. Teens and uncontrolled energy don't bode well," Disrayan said.

"That's why I need your help. I had already made plans before the fall of Ceres to establish a school for Aura youth outside of Ceres. A safe place for them to explore their energies and learn our history. Now more than ever, there is a need for such a school."

Zazzie went into the elevator pitch she had been working on for when she finally had a chance to officially approach the Ruling Council about her expanded idea. Disrayan was on the Council now, and although she was her friend, she would never act against the best interest of the Aura. This was Zazzie's chance to see if she was on the right track. In the middle of her speech, she received a text from Hendrex. She ignored it to get her point across, but then he called. She couldn't ignore that, but when she heard it wasn't anything important, she rushed him off the phone. He would understand, she hoped.

***

"What are you still doing here?" Jaq asked, peeking into Hendrex's office.

Hendrex looked up from his paperwork and scowled at his cousin.

"Working, what are you still doing here? Shouldn't you be home rubbing Enora's feet or something?"

Jaq laughed and invited himself into Hendrex's small office. Hendrex hadn't had a grand office back in Ceres, but this one was barely larger than Zarovia's closet at home. He wasn't complaining, though. This was the one space in the entire world that was truly his at this point. It had surprised him to have been voted in as Magistrate during the emergency elections, but not nearly as surprised that the people of Ceres had voted Jaquis Andromeda onto the Ruling Council.

"I didn't say you were welcome to stay. I am very busy, as you can see."

Jaq shrugged and propped himself against the arm of the chair across from Hendrex's desk.

"Enora is with the cackle right now, so we both have free time. Why you choose to work right now is beyond me. Let's go have a drink."

Hendrex briefly glanced at his phone. Zazzie hadn't mentioned being out late tonight when he'd texted her about dinner earlier. He picked up his phone and sent her a text. He didn't expect her to immediately answer, but after a few minutes of Jaq staring at him and making whip-like gestures in his direction, Hendrex decided to call her. This time she did answer.

"Is there an emergency?"

Hendrex scowled. That was definitely not the answer he expected.

"No, no, I just wanted to check in with you. See if we were still a go to have dinner at our usual time," he said.

Jaq doubled over in silent laughter.

"Oh right, I forgot we were doing the whole routine thing to help you adjust. I'm sorry, Hendrex, I'm with the girls right now. Don't wait up, okay?" Zazzie hung up before he could say anything else.

"Wow! How the mighty have fallen," Jaq gasped through his now unconstrained laughter.

Hendrex was livid, but he wouldn't give his cousin the satisfaction of knowing that, so he put on a smile and stacked the paperwork he had been going over neatly on his desk.

"Let's go have a drink," he said. "It may be the last time in a long while once the new curfew is in effect.

Jaq's smile widened, and he nodded. Hendrex stood and gestured for Jaq to go first. They were just shy of the front door when they ran into Icarus and Jasmine. Icarus Eridanus, once Hendrex's guard and now Ruling Three, looked like he'd rather be anywhere but in Jasmine's presence.

They'd garnered a sort of friendship since the fall of Ceres. Icarus had leaned on Hendrex in regard to learning about the Ruling Council and his new duties. Icarus was young and completely green in terms of politics, which was both a good thing and bad. He was idealistic enough to be open to change but too green to understand how to properly oppose the neigh-sayers. Which was why he needed rescue from Jasmine. She was, no doubt, badgering him about Council business in a way he wasn't prepared to handle.

"Hey man, you ready?" Jaq called out to him. Icarus smiled brightly and nodded.

"Uh yeah, excuse us, Jasmine. We have prior plans and can discuss this issue at a later date," Icarus said.

Jasmine raised an eyebrow at Icarus before turning a glare on Jaq.

"This isn't a matter that can be easily brushed aside. Since I have you and Jaq present, we can discuss this in earnest," she said.

Jaq shook his head.

"The Ruling Council is a 24/7 responsibility, but we need downtime as well, right, Hendrex? All work, no play makes a dull boy, am I right?"

Hendrex pinched the bridge of his nose before turning a warm smile on Jasmine. To be honest, Jasmine reminded him a lot of the late Ruling One. She was kind and intelligent, and she truly cared about the Aura. Sure, she could be a lot when trying to make a point, but she was often right.

"I think we can all agree you have had plenty of play and are by no means a dull boy. Anyway, Jasmine, would you like to join us for a drink? Think of it as a team-building exercise."

Jasmine smiled, and if Hendrex wasn't mistaken, even blushed a little.

"I guess a team builder could be in order."

"Seriously, Dre?" Jaq groaned.

"I'm cool with Jasmine joining us as long as we all agree not to talk business."

"As if I would risk exposing the Aura in a human

establishment," Jasmine scoffed.

"Then it's settled. Let's go," Hendrex said.

He started to walk off toward the nearby bar, and Jasmine caught up to him, looping her arm in his. His gut instinct was to pull away, but her grip tightened as a car whizzed by and his dedication to chivalry wouldn't allow him to.

"This will be my first time in a bar," she mumbled.

Hendrex nodded and gave her head a friendly pat.

"Don't worry, I'll make sure your first experience is a good one."

Thankfully, the bar wasn't far, and with it being the middle of the week, it wasn't crowded. Only a few regulars who typically kept to themselves graced the small space. Hendrex found their usual booth and ushered Jasmine inside. Jaq slid into the opposite side, and Icarus pushed Hendrex out of the way to sit next to Jasmine.

"So, what does one order to drink?" Jasmine asked.

Jaq got a mischievous grin on his face before signaling for the bartender.

"Don't worry, Jazz, I've got you."

Jasmine frowned.

"My name is Jasmine, not Jazz."

Icarus spoke up then.

"We all have what humans call nicknames that we use outside of Aura circles. Hendrex is Dre, Jaquis is Jaq, and I go by Rus. It helps us to remember we aren't completely amongst friends and keeps us from saying things we shouldn't," Icarus explained.

Jasmine seemed to contemplate it before nodding.

"Okay, then you can call me Jazz, but it might take a while for me to get used to this nickname thing."

It surprised Hendrex she didn't put up more of a fight about the name thing. He knew Jasmine was a stickler for tradition, and tradition meant that you were called by your given name. It was given for a reason, and to shorten it changed the meaning and weight carried by it.

Not for the first time, Hendrex wondered if Jasmine wouldn't be so rigid in her beliefs if she had been friends with Zazzie and the others. They'd all grown up together, even if Jasmine had chosen the path of an educator, instead of joining the Security Force like the girls had. Maybe if the girls saw Jasmine in this new light, they wouldn't be so harsh and stand-offish with her. Then again, they were a closed circuit. A fact Hendrex was getting to know very well. The anger that built with Zazzie's dismissal of him and their plans raged back to life.

The bartender brought over their usual round of beers, and Hendrex relaxed into the vinyl-covered bench seat as he took the first sip. The cool, bitter liquid the perfect foil to the molten frustration inside of him. Maybe after this beer, he would storm Farrah's apartment and drag Zazzie home like the males did in human stories. Maybe Zazzie would swoon and let him pleasure her for the rest of the evening like a male should. He snorted a laugh. Yeah, right. Zazzie would cuss his ass out and kick him out of her house, then Farrah would hex him, Disrayan would make what was left of his professional life a living hell, and Enora? Hendrex didn't even want to think of the ways Enora would destroy him over Zazzie.

No, it was best he swallow his pride on this and have a civil discussion about his feelings with her later. A clear head and calm heart were the best way to approach the situation, but the other option was damn tempting at the moment.

***

Disrayan took a sip of her tea and sighed. Zarovia could mentally see her putting her Ruling Council hat on as she formulated her response. "You're preaching to the choir, man. We know there is a need for a school. It's on the list of things to do, but right now, we are maxed out with trying to figure out how to make Langsmith a peaceful place again."

"Langsmith has never been peaceful," Farrah snorted.

Enora shrugged, "It was tense, for sure, but never like it is now."

"Like Ceres was ever the safest place? I mean, the lost ones were just one issue," Farrah supplied.

Zazzie could easily see the conversation getting lost in all the issues the Aura faced as a whole. She was just as concerned about it as the others, but she wasn't going to let them travel too far down that rabbit hole before she got the answers and support she needed from them.

"Can we stay on track here? I know having an entire school is going to take time. All I'm asking is for help with these two girls. Do you think there is any space at the Factory that could be used?"

Disrayan bit her lip and shook her head.

"The only free space right now is the equipment room, and that's not exactly safe for training."

"I can ask Jaq? He's been doing something similar with kids in The Resistance. He will know of places," Enora said.

"As long as Jaq doesn't try to get directly involved. Daphne isn't okay with The Resistance and won't want to train if she knows it's tied to them."

"I'll do my best, but we all know Jaq does as he pleases."

"Exactly, Andromeda men," Disrayan lamented.

"Oh no! You are not allowed to go in on Andromeda men after getting married without letting any of us know first!"

Disrayan rolled her eyes at Enora.

"Says the woman who got knocked up by one without telling us either."

Zazzie shook her head.

"Look, we can all go round-robin on the Andromeda penchant for being stubborn, or we can have an actually productive conversation, like when are we having Disrayan's party, or Enora's baby shower, and how we are going to get Farrah to the Binding Ceremony with the least number of casualties?"

That garnered a laugh from everyone but Farrah, who downed the last of her wine before pouring herself another glass. She didn't get a chance to drink it as Donovan waltzed through the door.

"We've got a situation at the Greywulf compound. Sorry to interrupt your girl's night."

"Ugh, of course. There can't be a single night to relax," Farrah muttered, but excitement danced in her eyes.

Shaking her head, Zazzie grabbed her purse.

"Are we all needed?"

"I don't know yet. I'm sure Farrah will keep you all posted."

With that, they were all shuffled out of the apartment so Donovan and Farrah could lock up and be on their way.

"I can drive you both home," Enora offered.

"No, I need the walk to clear my head. Plus, I wanted to go by the Factory and talk with a few of the kids there."

Disrayan shook her head. "Shouldn't you be rushing home to be with your Andromeda?"

Zazzie bit her lip. She did feel bad for being dismissive of Hendrex earlier, but she couldn't relax and enjoy her evening with him when she was so worried about the kids.

"I already told him I would be home late, and he will understand when I explain it was for the children. I don't think Daphne is the only one picking fights on the streets."

Disrayan and Enora exchanged looks before shrugging at each other.

"I doubt that, as well, but as a concerned friend, sometimes work needs to take a back seat. Enora, I'll take the ride. It's been a long day, and I could use the rest if we aren't needed for this latest drama," Disrayan said.

"I'm sure we will know soon if we are needed or not," Enora said, and it was clear she hoped not. Zazzie couldn't blame her. Being as pregnant as she was, Enora wouldn't be able to help out, and it would only mean a long night worrying about Jaq.

"Have a good evening otherwise, ladies."

Zarovia headed in the direction of the Factory. Farrah's apartment was only a few blocks from the Aura headquarters. What had once been the secret entrance to Ceres now acted as a ramshackle version of the once Great Sanctuary. There were several families still sleeping on huddled cots in the various rooms of the Factory. She paid a visit to each one. Talking to the kids, asking how they were adjusting.

She hoped more of the older kids would have started at the schools, but it was taking longer to come up with the necessary paperwork for them under the current situation. It also didn't help that Jasmine Hyperion, an instructor from Ceres, was adamant about maintaining the traditional teachings while also being adamant against any real socialization of the children to their new home. Zarovia knew any talks of opening a school for the Aura would bring her into the fold, but Zazzie wasn't mentally prepared to deal with the woman. At least, not right then. One thing was certain. She was going to need every bit of capital she'd already raised and then some to make this dream a reality.

***

"Earth to Hendrex." Icarus raised his hand in front of Hendrex's face. Apparently, he'd been lost in thought and had missed something important. He glanced down at the table and cursed. It was littered with bottles. Four of them in front of him, and yet he didn't feel buzzed in the slightest.

"Sorry, did you ask me something?"

Icarus raised his eyebrow and nodded towards Jasmine, who was blushing furiously and not in an embarrassed way. She had two bottles in front of her along with three shot glasses. How had he missed her taking shots? He was doing a poor job of his promise to keep her safe.

He glared at Jaq, the only person who would order shots for someone not used to drinking. He shrugged and had the nerve to look unbothered by the whole situation.

"I think she is allergic to alcohol," Jaq whispered to Hendrex.

"You think? Call Enora and tell her to meet us at the Factory."

Hendrex was out of his seat and around to help with Jasmine, who was already leaning precariously to one side.

"I've got her," Icarus offered as he slid out of the seat, pulling Jasmine along with him. Hendrex shook his head.

"I promised to take care of her. I'll make sure she gets back to the Factory."

Icarus shrugged and shook his head.

"Your funeral, bro."

"What?"

"I've got the tab, you guys go ahead," Icarus said.

As soon as Icarus let go of Jasmine's other arm, she nearly fell. Hendrex cursed and lifted her into his arms. He didn't think twice before taking off out of the bar and down the street. Jasmine snuggled closer to him, her eyes glassy and unfocused.

"Hendrex," she said in a voice that sounded almost like a purr. She wiggled, rubbing her chest against him and making it hard for him to hold her steady.

"Jasmine, please," he said, shifting her weight again. They were only one block from the Factory now. Jaq was beside him on the phone with a pissed-off Enora.

Hendrex could tell her mood by the fact Jaq was holding the phone away from his ear, and Enora was definitely not okay with being called out when she was just about to slip into a bath. Which then turned into another argument entirely because, apparently, it was unsafe for her at this stage to do so alone.

"Baby, think of the baby! What if something happens and I'm not there to take care of you?" Jaq said.

"Then your ass should have been at home instead of at a fucking bar," Enora snapped.

Hendrex tuned both out, returning his focus to Jasmine. She was still purring and rubbing her chest against him. If it had been any other situation, Hendrex would have put her down and made her walk. The walk to the Factory was short but would have helped work the alcohol out of her system faster.

Jaq opened the door for them, and Hendrex carried Jasmine into the makeshift medical office. He gently placed Jasmine on the table, and she giggled, pressing feather-light kisses on any piece of exposed skin she could manage to reach. Hendrex made a note to never let Jasmine drink again. Not even for ritual purposes.

"I've always dreamed of you putting me to bed, under different circumstances, of course."

Hendrex shook his head and chose to ignore her comment. She was in medical peril. Nothing she said right now was worth pondering over. For all he knew, she thought he was Icarus or another more single Aura male. He let go of her and turned to leave. Jaq arguing with Enora was bound to delay her getting there.

Jasmine grabbed his arm and pulled him roughly back to her. He tripped over his feet and landed right on top of her. Before he could correct the situation, Jasmine's lips were on his. She moaned with delight, grabbing Hendrex's shirt in the balls of her tiny fists.

"Please don't go, stay with me, make me yours," Jasmine moaned against his lips.

It was time for him to go, only it was too late to pretend none of this ever happened. He sensed Zazzie's shock and anger in a wave of scalding hot energy before she even spoke.

"The fuck!"

Hendrex froze at the sound of Zazzie's voice. He forced himself away from Jasmine and turned to Zazzie, who glared angrily at him. Jasmine sat up and pouted.

"Ugh, here you are to ruin things, as usual," Jasmine said.

Zazzie looked ready to fight, but just as she took a step toward them, Enora rushed in.

"Oh good, she isn't unconscious. Hendrex, please get her a glass of water."

Hendrex took the opportunity to get farther away from Jasmine as he went to the Factory cafeteria to get said glass of water. Zazzie followed.

***

"If this wasn't a monogamous thing, you should

have said so from the beginning," she snapped as soon as they were alone.

Hendrex pulled her into his arms and cupped her chin, bringing her gaze to meet his. The fact she didn't immediately pull away or feel the urge to slap the shit out of him told her she wasn't as mad as she thought. She was heartbroken.

Damn it, I'm in love with him.

It was the only explanation as to why she would have bothered following him or even be willing to listen to what he had to say. Hell, she'd broken up with others for much less serious offenses. She'd practically caught Hendrex about to fuck Jasmine, of all people, and here she was chasing after him like she had done something wrong. This was not her usual self at all.

"I'm sorry, Zazzie. I promise you nothing happened between me and Jasmine. Nothing will ever happen between her and me. You are the only woman I want."

"That doesn't explain everything."

"No, it doesn't, but I hope you trust me enough to know I would never do anything to hurt you."

Zazzie turned away from him and filled a glass with water.

"I'll take this to Enora. You, go home. We'll talk more about this later."

Zazzie stormed off before Hendrex could say another word. Her anger returned the moment she set foot back in the small clinic and saw Jasmine refusing Enora's help. When Jasmine pushed Enora, Zazzie lost it. She tossed the water in Jasmine's face.

"Bitch, touch her again and see what happens!"

Jasmine shrieked in rage and wiped at her face.

"You again! You're just mad that Hendrex finally saw what a hag you are and came to me for comfort," Jasmine spat.

Sick or not, Zazzie wasn't going to let that go. She lunged for Jasmine, catching hold of her hair and dragging her off the table. Jasmine grabbed a fist full of Zazzie's locs as she fell, pulling Zazzie down with her. Zazzie hauled back, ready to knock the mess out of her, but thought better of it at the last second and let her fist open, landing an open-handed blow across the woman's already reddened cheeks.

Jasmine shrieked and pulled Zazzie's hair even harder. One of Zazzie's locs broke, the tiny bell attached to it tinkling as it hit the floor beside her. Angered even more that her hair had been damaged, Zazzie forgot about propriety. She grabbed Jasmine by the throat with one hand and brought the other hand back to punch her for real when Jaq grabbed her from behind and dragged her away. She didn't fight Jaq as he dragged her to Hendrex's office and blocked the door so she couldn't escape and resume venting her anger on Jasmine.

"You done, or do I need to call Mack to come drain your energy?" he said.

"I'm sure as hell not done. She fucking pushed Enora!"

"That really why you fought her?"

Zazzie could feel Jaq's energy probing around in her head, and she picked up a pen from Hendrex's desk and threw it at him.

"Stay out of my head, asshole!"

Jaq smirked as he apparently found what he was looking for in her head. She could feel his energy receding.

"Go home, talk to Hendrex and go easy on him, okay? He's had you on the brain all day, and this shit with Jasmine was all one-sided. I promise."

With that, Jaq motioned for Zazzie to go. She left the office, and he followed.

"You don't have to escort me out. I know the way," she said.

"Uh, yeah, I do. You were lucky I could shield everyone from your little anger spike. No one will know what happened who wasn't in the room when it did."

Zazzie flicked him off, but when they reached the front doors of the Factory, she turned around and gave him a brief hug.

"Thank you, and tell Enora I'm sorry, okay? I know how she is around violence."

Jaq nodded and turned around. Begrudgingly, Zazzie took the long way home. She needed time to cool off and get her head together. On her trip, she passed by Club Obelisk. It wasn't on the way to her place, but she was still too worked up to go home, and Club Obelisk was the only safe place to be at night. A mandatory neutral ground set in place by the owner, Molly.

Mack was working the bar, and he placed a shot in front of her as soon as she reached the bar.

"Jaq filled me in by text. I'll keep them coming until you tell me you've had enough or you're too drunk to make it home safely," Mack said and walked away.

Zazzie raised a toast to his back and downed the blood-red liquid. It was surprisingly sweet and tasted of sour cherry before filling her throat with a warmth that relaxed her almost instantly. Disrayan wasn't happy with Mack's chosen profession, but making drinks like this? Zazzie was sure this was his true passion and not any of this whole undercover garbage he'd been spouting when he first came back to the fold.

Mack dropped another shot for her as he passed, and after she downed it, she realized she wasn't alone. Molly had propped her petite, redheaded-self right beside her.

"I know that look," Molly said.

"What look?"

"The 'I'm about to kill a bitch for touching my man' look," she laughed.

Zazzie rolled her eyes.

"She pushed my pregnant best friend."

"Is she still alive? If not, I can arrange a quiet disappearance."

Zazzie couldn't help but laugh, even as Molly's words sent an uneasy chill down her spine. Zazzie didn't know much about Molly, other than the fact that she was somehow Aura and Vampire, and her Vampire sire was the bogeyman of many of her people's folk tales. There was no reason to trust Molly. Mack was, for whatever reason, loyal to the woman. Maybe for tonight, that could be enough.

"As tempting as that sounds, I can't sanction a hit on one of the Ruling Council. We've already lost too much."

Molly looked like she was desperate to ask more questions, but instead, signaled Mack to bring them another round of drinks.

"What's your poison tonight, boss?" Mack asked.

Molly smiled. "A Bloody Mary, please, and have the server bring our drinks to VIP. Zazzie is my special guest this evening."

Mack raised an eyebrow before doing as ordered. Molly looped her arm in Zazzie's and brought her to the raised platform designated for VIPs. From the main floor, you couldn't see the soundproof glass between each section of booths.

"Vampires have exceptional hearing," Molly said, leading her to a booth in the far back with a black sound dampening curtain. Once there, Zazzie could hear none of the commotion outside, only the music pumping through unseen speakers.

"This is actually pretty cool," Zazzie said.

"Only the best for my VIPs. Anyway, this is a safe

place, okay? So, feel free to talk or not, scream, cry. Whatever you need," Molly said. The server appeared and brought them their drinks. Molly took hers and turned to leave, but Zazzie grabbed her arm.

"Stay. I don't think I'll be comfortable alone."

Molly smiled.

"Sure." Molly sat in one of the blood-red velvet seats and sipped at her cocktail.

Zazzie realized she suddenly had so many questions, but she was too afraid to ask. She knew practically nothing about Vampires.

Molly noticed her curiosity and smiled.

"How about we play three truths and a lie? I'm sure we both have a million questions about each other, and I'm an open book."

Zazzie considered her words before nodding.

"Sure, why not?"

***

Should Molly feel bad about plying Zarovia with alcohol to get her to talk? Yes. Did she feel bad? No. Besides, Zazzie seemed like she really needed to work out whatever was bothering her with a neutral party.

"I'll go first," Molly offered.

"I am an orphan, I have never had sex in my club, I hate my red hair, and fairy tale romance is a crock of shit."

Zazzie seemed to ponder the answer before shaking her head.

"Your hair is gorgeous; how could you hate it? That's the lie."

"Drink. My workspace is sacred."

Zazzie downed her shot and stared at the ceiling.

"I don't think it is fair to play with you. You are a Vampire. Can't you tell when people are lying?"

"I promise not to cheat and use my Vampire abilities, now come on."

Zazzie took another shot.

"I have amazing friends, I value freedom of expression, my life's dream is to open a school that is safe for the Supernatural children of Langsmith to learn and grow, and I wish Jasmine Hyperion gets herpes from the first human she fucks."

"I'm assuming this Jasmine is part of the reason you are here, but I don't think you could truly wish anyone harm."

"Fine, but if I were that petty, she would definitely be first on the list. Not only did she try to seduce my man, but she pushed my pregnant best friend."

Zazzie took a shot, and Molly took a shot too.

"Okay, so maybe there weren't any lies in your set."

Both women laughed.

"I bet you don't have any troubles with your mate. I hear Vampires are quite single-minded with those they care for."

Molly snorted.

"Yes, but that doesn't mean I haven't had to scare off my share of women from my Shane."

"Ugh, I guess all men are stupid."

"Yeah, they are."

Molly grabbed the last two shots on the tray just as Gretchen brought in a fresh tray of shots.

"What are we toasting too?" Gretchen said, taking a shot of her own.

"Men who are too stupid to stay out of situations with women not their mates," Zazzie said.

Gretchen laughed.

"I'll toast to that." The three women clinked drinks and downed their shots.

Hendrex paced the living room of Zazzie's home. She hadn't arrived yet, despite Jaq assuring he sent her home hours ago. He'd tried calling her, but she hadn't answered her phone either. He looked at his phone for what seemed like the hundredth time that night and still nothing.

"Come on, Zazzie, where are you?"

He went to the kitchen and busied himself with fixing a cup of tea. He needed something to help calm his nerves, but he would not raid Zazzie's stash of medicinal herbs to do so. He would have to settle for herbal tea instead.

He needed what little wits he had left to have the conversation with Zazzie he knew was coming. He downed the tea he made, not caring that it was scorching hot and burned the mess out of his tongue and throat. He was too anxious about Zazzie. He picked up his phone again and saw he had a text from Mack.

M: Zazzie's at Obelisk.

With a curse, Hendrex dropped his cup and ran out the door. Club Obelisk was the last place an Aura female should be. She may be safe inside, but as soon as she set foot outside, Hendrex didn't want to think of it.

It didn't matter that he didn't have a car. He ran all the way there, and for once, was glad that he and his brother were identical. While they may dress differently, the bouncer hadn't been able to tell the difference and let him right in.

"Where is she?" he demanded as soon as he reached the bar.

Mack looked up at him and shook his head.

"I never in a million years thought I'd be pouring Zazzie drinks because you fucking cheated on her.

You're lucky I'm good at mixing energy with my potions; otherwise, she would have burnt what little shit you own to the ground," Mack said.

"Just tell me where she is."

Mack waved over a brunette with a scarf; Hendrex thought she looked familiar but couldn't put a name or chance encounter to the face.

"Gretchen, can you escort my brother to the VIP?"

Gretchen glared at Hendrex before flashing her fangs at him.

"I don't help cheaters."

"I didn't cheat. It was a misunderstanding," Hendrex argued.

"I can smell the other woman on you."

Hendrex opened his mouth to speak, but Claude came sauntering over and draped a protective arm over Gretchen's shoulder.

"Hendrex, I see you've met my mate." There was an edge to Claude's voice, and Hendrex knew he needed to tread lightly, no matter how infuriating the situation was.

"Evening, Claude, may you please ask your mate to escort me to mine so I can handle some personal business?"

Claude made a face before looking down at Gretchen. She glared up at him and shook her head.

"Sorry, no can do," Claude said.

"For fuck's sake," Hendrex cursed.

"Hendrex? What are you doing here?"

Zazzie's voice was like music to his ears. He tried to move around Gretchen and Claude to get to her, but both Vampires were faster than him and blocked his way. Gretchen turned to Zazzie and gripped her shoulders.

"Tell me you don't want to talk to this asshat, and he's gone."

Zazzie smiled softly and shook her head.

"No, we need to talk, just not here. Thank you all for being so kind to me, but I should call it a night."

Zazzie gave Molly and Gretchen both hugs before heading toward the door. Hendrex had no choice but to follow. She didn't speak until they reached her car, which was still parked in front of Farrah's apartment building.

"I thought you weren't mad at me. I thought you wanted to talk?" he said, sliding into the driver's seat since he hadn't been the one drinking.

Zazzie stared out the window.

"I do, and I'm not. I just needed time to figure shit out, okay? I don't do this. I don't get jealous over men. Especially ones who aren't committed to me."

"Not committed? Zazzie."

She put her hand up, stopping him.

"Don't. We've never really talked about what we are doing here. Things just started happening, and something like this was bound to occur sooner or later. I honestly don't have the bandwidth for any of it right now. Can we just go home? I'm tired."

Hendrex wanted to press the issue, but if he was honest, he was tired too, and she was already shut down. He could feel her building walls between them that had never been there before. Even when they actively denied their attraction to one another.

Wronged

Zazzie's head hurt. She'd definitely drank too much the night before. At least, she had all the ingredients in her kitchen to make herself a potent hangover cure so she could make it safely to work that morning. Still, she had zero tolerance for BS. Darnell had been moved to the other side of the building, so at least he wouldn't bother her. But the rumor mill in the office was running strong. Zazzie couldn't wait until she had her school and she could leave this place behind. She just had to get through the rest of the morning and lunch with the girls.

Of course, Enora had raised the alarm, and an emergency meeting had been called to discuss the Jasmine situation. Honestly, Zazzie didn't want to talk about it, but that didn't mean she wouldn't have to, at least for today.

Zazzie did her best to wrap up most of her work for the day, choosing to spend time between the schools instead of stuck in her office all day. Then she headed out. They were meeting at Enora's this time, since Jaq had basically put Enora on bed rest after Jasmine had pushed her.

"I'm here," Zazzie announced herself as she walked

into Enora's.

She was the last to arrive, and Enora had already set out tea and cookies that were half-eaten.

"Finally, I was about to come drag your ass over here so you can tell us what the hell happened," Farrah said.

Zazzie plopped onto Enora's couch and sighed.

"Enora didn't tell you?"

"She did, but we want to hear it from you," Disrayan said.

"Jasmine pushed Enora. I wasn't going to let her get away with that," Zazzie said.

Farrah snorted, "Gotcha, but what about my whack ass cousin?"

"What about him?"

"So, it's over then? You really are going to walk away because of Jasmine?" Disrayan shook her head.

"Fuck no, I meant that there is nothing to discuss. Jasmine overstepped, and she's been put in her place. Besides, things with Hendrex and I are complicated as it is. The last thing I'm worried about with him is another woman."

Her friends exchanged looks over their teacups.

"What?"

"Complicated? He lives with you," Disrayan said.

"*He* needed a place to stay. He's a friend. I help my friends."

"Oh my god, and I thought Disrayan was the delusional one when it came to her feelings for Mack," Farrah said.

Disrayan tossed a cookie at Farrah, who caught it and shoved it in her mouth with a big grin.

"I am not delusional! We just haven't had that talk yet," Zazzie clarified.

"Even worse," Enora groaned, "I am speaking from

experience when I say that undefined relationships are not a thing."

"I don't even understand how that is possible. Hendrex isn't the type to enter anything without hashing out all the minute details," Disrayan said.

Zazzie bit her lip. Rye was right. Their whole situation didn't fit with Hendrex's personality. Maybe that's why Jasmine had felt so sure of herself in courting him. She was a staunch traditionalist, just like he was. She shook the thought away.

If Hendrex wanted to be with another woman, he wouldn't be in her house.

"Ugh, this is pointless. Whatever is going on between Hendrex and I is our business." Zazzie stood and left. Not caring that she hadn't touched the tea or cookies or that she was super rude to her friends.

Disrayan caught her by the door.

"Zazzie, wait!"

Zazzie stopped and turned around.

"What, Rye? I have to get back to work."

"Don't be mad at us because you and Hendrex haven't figured your shit out. That's not entirely why we called you here today. I wanted to let you know that Jaq, Icarus, and I have approved the use of the Factory for your classes. It's not the ideal space, but we understand your need for a safe place for the kids to practice."

Zazzie smiled brightly and threw her arms around her.

"Ahh, that's amazing news, thank you!"

"I'm glad you're happy. Now, get to work, and please, for all our sake, define your shit with Hendrex."

***

Hendrex Andromeda was avoiding her. Jasmine wasn't sure what exactly had happened the night she

83

went with him and the others to the bar, but none of them would look her in the eye. Jaq had hinted about what happened, but she couldn't take him seriously. He claimed she got into a physical fight with Zarovia Monoceros, of all people, and had kissed Hendrex! There was no way she would have done any of those things. Then again, judging by everyone's reaction to her, maybe she had. At least, they had the decency to keep it amongst themselves. The Aura community was small and gossip rampant. The last thing Jasmine needed was for her reputation to be so irreparably tarnished.

Hendrex rounded the corner and waved off one of the teens who was talking to him about something Jasmine couldn't quite make out. He was, no doubt, on his way to his office. Not to be caught staring after the man, Jasmine ducked between a set of machinery. She watched from the safety of the shadowed hallway as Hendrex Andromeda strode confidently to his office.

She bit her lip to keep from swooning as brief shafts of light filtering in through the rows of machinery flashed across the rippling muscles of his arms. While Jasmine wasn't a fan of most human things, seeing the way their clothing hugged and highlighted his powerful frame gave her something she could like about them. A flash of memory interrupted her train of thought. Her gripping desperately to Hendrex and pressing kisses along the very flesh she currently ogled. Her face heated, and she buried her face in her hands. Had she really done that?

"Ms. Hyperion?"

Jasmine nearly jumped out of her shoes as one of her teenage students startled her. She quickly corrected her posture and fixed her face into a neutral expression.

"Yes, Mr. Cassian?"

Only her students could call her Ms. Hyperion and only when the issue they wished to discuss was about their school work. Balancing the role of Ruling Council and educator was difficult, but she would have it no other way. None of the other educators in Ceres had made it to safety and stuck around after the initial attacks. She was the only one left to carry on the Aura instructional traditions.

"Sorry to startle you. I just wanted to ask if I could miss class this evening. Ms. Monoceros is teaching a defensive energies class I would like to take as well."

Jasmine frowned. Zarovia Monoceros was the bane of her existence. The living embodiment of the worst-case scenario of any sane Aura parent. An Aura so lost in the human culture she'd even adopted their bastardized energy practices as her own. Not to mention, she currently held the attention of Hendrex Andromeda.

"No, you may not be excused," she huffed and started to walk away but thought she may need to drive her point home with the teen and paused.

"And if any of your fellow students wish to opt-out of tonight's class, tell them not to return. I cannot teach proper Aura traditions if you are being taught the exact opposite by someone who has no common decency. I will be speaking to the parents about this."

With that, she left the teen stunned in her wake. Jasmine didn't like being harsh with the children, but that was how things were done. It was the only way things were done. If you gave children an inch, they would take a mile. Zarovia Monoceros and her friends were the ultimate proof of that. The only one of the four women who had any decency was Disrayan, and even she had been corrupted by her so-called friends.

Jasmine herself had almost fallen victim to these radical notions of a new Aura identity. Maybe it was her attraction to Hendrex Andromeda that had blinded her to the treasonous acts of the others, but no longer could she stand by and watch her people's traditions fall to the wayside. Now that Aura no longer had the Sanctuary and almost all of their historical record was lost, it was up to those who knew the proper way to keep traditions going.

It was up to people like Jasmine, and she would not back down this time. She would not be swayed. Not even by the sexy as sin Hendrex Andromeda. She would be strong for her people and for their traditions. She settled in her office and made the preparations. She had begrudgingly approved Zarovia spearheading the creation of a school for Aura children. It wasn't that there wasn't a need for it. Surely there was, however, Zarovia Monoceros was not the person to run it. Maybe when it was simply children already corrupted by human ideals, but not for the true innocents. Those who had never set foot outside of Ceres before now. Jasmine wasn't sure how, but she knew she needed to stop whatever Zarovia planned to do.

Somehow, she would take control of the school and banish Zarovia Monoceros from any importance in Aura history.

****

Daphne and Sarah stood on opposite sides of the room that had been cleared for Zazzie's defensive arts class, the first official class of what Zazzie hoped to one day call the Aura Academy. This wasn't their first meeting. They had attempted classes in different locations around Langsmith, but none had felt safe enough. Finally, Zazzie had gotten approval from the Ruling Council to use space in the Factory. Well, not the entire Council, Jasmine Hyperion was staunchly against anything to do with Zazzie, and after the other night, Zazzie knew the reason. Before, she had assumed Jasmine was just set in her ways. Now, she knew the animosity between

86

them all these years had stemmed more from Zazzie's relationship with Hendrex than anything logical.

Jasmine had always had a stick up her ass a mile long. She was immovable in her thinking, and it was that rigidity that Zazzie assumed most people had clung to in their uncertain times. Still, Zazzie never thought Jasmine would be such a bitch because of a man. With a sigh, Zazzie shook her head. She never thought she would fight a woman over a man either, and yet, that had happened as well. Zazzie had felt off balance and unsure of herself ever since Hendrex took an active role in her life.

"Are we waiting for others to come? I know a few kids said they were interested but weren't sure they could make it," Daphne said, drawing Zazzie's attention back to the task at hand.

Zazzie checked the clock on the wall. It was almost time for class to start. She'd opened the training to other children and teens, but as Daphne had pointed out, it seemed no one else planned to come.

"Alright, I guess we should get started."

Zazzie needed to focus. It had taken a lot of string-pulling to get the Ruling Council to agree to clear this space for her. Not because they didn't believe in what she was trying to do, but because space at the Factory was limited. Jaq could have provided an alternative space but nothing as secure.

The Council wouldn't have approved of any Aura practicing their energies out in the open, anyway. Especially now, as any such activity would draw the unwanted attention of the Rogue Vampires intent on establishing dominance and chaos in the area. Now that it was common knowledge Aura blood made Vampires more powerful, the youth were at more risk of being attacked and abducted for showing their strength in energy knowledge.

"Are we going to learn how to throw energy daggers or something useful?" Sarah asked.

Daphne shot Sarah a disgusted look, but Zazzie could tell that even Daphne was excited about the possibility. They were both going to be sadly disappointed with today's lesson. Not only were energy daggers not a thing Zazzie felt she would ever teach them, but she wasn't up for much more than the basics of energy manipulation.

"Today, we'll start with the basics," Zazzie said, "First, you must learn to identify the energy around you. Without knowledge of the surrounding energy, you can never learn to control it."

"How do you recognize energies?" said Sarah.

"You must be in touch with your inner energy, and to do that, you'll have to learn to sit in silence and meditate."

"This is baby stuff! I thought we were here to learn how to control our new energy, not the things that we were born knowing," said Daphne.

"Speak for yourself," said Sarah. "Ms. Zazzie, can you please continue? I would like to learn more."

"Of course, you do. You're new to this energy thing," said Daphne, "I don't even know why you're here."

Sarah balled up her fists and stalked toward Daphne. "We both wouldn't be here if it wasn't for your reckless behavior."

Normally, Zazzie would be content to let the girls sort out their differences on their own, but things were quickly getting out of hand. Zazzie stepped between the two girls and put her hands up.

"Both of you are here for a reason. Sarah needs to learn to use energy. Daphne, so do you, your education in your energies is lacking, although, you may have more intuitive knowledge than Sarah at the moment."

Daphne smirked at Sarah, but Zazzie wasn't about to let the girl think she was any better than Sarah in any way. They needed to learn they were equals before they could effectively work as a team. She thought they had come to some sort of truce, since she'd seen them hanging in the same groups more recently. Zazzie wasn't trying to train them to fight. That wasn't her goal. She wanted them to be able to effectively control their energies and protect themselves if necessary.

"Sarah is well trained in the defensive arts, and Daphne, you can learn a lot from her in that regard. I am simply here to facilitate the learning process and offer guidance when necessary. I don't want this to be a punishment. I want this to be a learning experience that you guys can take into the outside world to be safe."

There was a slow clap from the doorway to the room. Zazzie spun around, excited that they had at least one more participant, but her smile faltered as soon as she saw the redhead standing in the doorway.

"That was an amazing speech," Molly said.

Zazzie felt Daphne tense behind her. Her frantic energy whipped around the room, snapping at Zazzie's skin like tiny rubber bands. She turned her head to make sure Daphne wasn't preparing to strike, thankfully Sarah had a firm grip on Daphne's arm, keeping her in place while offering a small amount of comfort. Molly was a Vampire, and that had to be triggering for Daphne. Zazzie turned back to Molly, who stood hesitantly in the doorway. Molly's eyes sparkled with wariness, but it wasn't Zazzie's job to make the woman more comfortable here. Her job was to protect Daphne.

"Hi, Molly, is there something I can do for you?"

Molly gave her head an almost imperceptible shake before she smiled widely, revealing her fangs. Sarah hissed, and before Zazzie could react, Daphne flared violently before charging at Molly. Sarah was already mid-shift, and that meant Zazzie had to act fast. Zazzie attempted to catch the Sarah before she got too close, but it was no use. Sarah slipped right through her fingers, and the despite the quickness of each move the girl made, the world seemed to slow as both Daphne and Molly prepared to defend themselves.

This moment would undoubtedly be make or break for Zazzie's hopes of opening an all-inclusive school. There was no telling what Molly would do. Any altercation between her and Daphne would be unacceptable and lead to a huge mess that would leave more than just Zazzie out in the cold. Daphne stopped dead in her tracks as Molly glowed with energy.

"I'm not the one who hurt you, child." Molly's voice didn't sound like her own. It resonated as if multiple people spoke at once. Daphne struggled against Molly's energy, but it made little difference. Molly was stronger than Daphne.

"Go to hell, Vamp!" Daphne spit.

Molly shrugged, the layering of her voice disappearing as the glow softened around her.

"Been there, done that. Look, I'm here to train as well. I know when you mentioned starting this class it wasn't exactly an invitation, but I feel bad taking up so much of Mack's time."

She was powering down, and Zazzie was grateful. The amount of energy she'd been throwing off would have alerted others in the building that things had gotten out of hand, and that was the last thing she needed.

Zazzie pinched the bridge of her nose. She knew it had been a bad idea to mention her class during their game of three truths and a lie. It wasn't that Zazzie didn't want to help Molly, and Disrayan would definitely appreciate the extra time with Mack. The problem was Daphne.

Molly was a Vampire, and Daphne hated Vampires. One day she hoped Daphne wouldn't condemn all Vampires, but based on all of their experiences, trusting a Vampire was very hard to do.

"I don't think that's a good idea."

Sarah snorted.

"It's a terrible idea! One uncontrolled Aura is enough. Molly, you are too dangerous," Sarah said.

Molly's eyes narrowed at the young Shifter.

"Of all people, I thought you would understand. Being two different things at once isn't easy."

"Yeah, but at least, for me, if I lose control, the most that will happen is a few people get tossed around. Your energy literally vaporizes people and disrupts entire regions of Supernaturals and their abilities."

"This is not the time or the place for this. Molly, I understand you would like to train with us, but obviously, that isn't going to work out. We can schedule for another time, please."

Molly shifted her attention back to Zazzie. "Fine, I will be in touch."

With that, she pivoted on her heels and sauntered out of the room. Once she was gone, the tension evaporated, and everyone visibly sagged with relief.

"This whole idea is stupid. I'm out of here," Daphne said and marched out before Zazzie could stop her.

With a sigh, Zazzie turned to Sarah.

"Are you going to bail on this too?"

Sarah shook her head.

"I want to learn."

***

Jasmine wrapped up her evening class early. The kids were distracted, and so was she. She did not know Zarovia had been given access to one of the spaces at the

Factory for this defensive energy course. Of course, no one was really telling her anything at the moment. They were all too busy avoiding her because of what happened. Jasmine wasn't about to be shut out on this. She would just peek her head in, see if Zarovia was doing what she was supposed to be.

Jasmine disliked the woman with a passion, but she didn't entirely disagree with the children learning to protect themselves, especially after the attack on Ceres. She was just saying goodbye to the last lingering child when she saw a red-haired woman walking down the hall. Concerned about a breach in security, Jasmine followed. The woman made a direct path to the place Zarovia was holding her unsanctioned class. Teaching Daphne to control herself was one thing. Inviting a Vampire into their midst was another. Jasmine reached the room just as a wave of energy immobilized her. She could do nothing more than stand just outside the door and listen as Zarovia confirmed Jasmine's fears.

Not only did Zarovia plan to teach Aura children, but she planned to teach others as well. At least, it seemed Daphne had a better head on her shoulders than her supposed instructor. Freed from the invisible hold, Jasmine ducked behind a row of machinery in time to see both Daphne and the redheaded Vampire leave.

Serves Zarovia right. How dare she risk exposing our safe house to outsiders!

Jasmine was ready to give Zarovia a piece of her mind but stopped in her tracks when she saw Zarovia was still not alone.

"What the hell is going on here? I thought your class was to teach Aura youth! What the hell are you doing with a Shifter girl?"

Zarovia whirled around and glared at Jasmine.

"What I do in my class is none of your concern."

"Actually, it is, considering you are in our community space."

"Space I asked permission to use and was granted said permission."

"Yet your use of the space is unsanctioned. I demand you leave!"

Zarovia cocked her head to the side and sucked her teeth.

"You really want to start another fight with me, Jasmine?"

She felt Zarovia gathering her energy. Jasmine may have fought her before, but she had been drunk and beside herself. Even then, she stood no chance against a trained Security Force Officer, even a failed one. With a huff, Jasmine spun on her heels and marched out of the room. She heard Zarovia and the Shifter girl laughing at her as she left.

This is far from over, Zarovia Monoceros!

Jasmine didn't need to resort to brute force to get her way. She had brains and a position of power amongst her people. She strode into the refuge quarters and gathered as many parents as she could.

"Dear parents. I regret to have to inform you that Zarovia Monoceros can no longer be trusted with our children. At this very moment, I saw with my very own eyes her exposing the secrets of the Aura, not just to a Shifter girl who has yet to truly prove herself an ally, but also to a Vampire."

A collective gasp came from the crowd.

"She brought a Vampire into our refuge."

"Why hasn't this been discussed by the Ruling Council?"

Jasmine clapped her hands to bring their attention back to her.

"As you all know, despite the previous Ruling

Three's atrocious behavior, he warned us of the alliances formed by the Andromeda and Mars family. As a close friend to the Andromedas, it seems Ms. Monoceros' behavior will remain unchecked unless the public demands justice for her crimes. I cannot let this stand, and as concerned citizens and parents, I hope you will all join me in bringing Ms. Monoceros to justice."

A few of the parents wandered away, but most of the crowd stayed to listen to her plan. She wasn't worried about the others. She just hoped they would someday see the light. Ceres may have fallen, but their ideals must not.

***

"What a bitch," Sarah said.

Normally, Zazzie would correct her use of foul language, but she was technically off the clock, so she let it slide.

"Well, after that interruption, we have about 30 minutes left of our class time. I should be able to help you connect with your inner energy in that time."

Zazzie grabbed two of the three yoga mats she had brought with her and laid them out facing one another. She sat in a cross-legged position on the mat and gestured for Sarah to join her.

Sarah mimicked her positioning.

"Okay, now what?"

"Close your eyes and focus on your breathing."

Zazzie waited until she heard Sarah find a steady rhythm to her breath.

"No, take your hands and rub them together. Feel the heat building in your palms."

Zazzie let her eyes flutter open. She could connect with her energy later. Right now, she wanted to make sure Sarah was doing what she asked.

Sarah lifted her hands and rubbed them together.

"Focus on the heat. Imagine the heat as light between your palms."

Zazzie waited. This was all a visualization exercise; she didn't expect for any energy to truly manifest itself, but slowly, energy visibly snapped back and forth between Sarah's palms. Like tiny arcs of static electricity.

"Now try to follow that light to its source. Examine your body, notice which sectors are lit up as well. What colors you see as you follow the path of energy to your core energy."

The white arcs settled into a softly glowing orb between the girl's hands, the color-shifting from white to red, to green, then blue. It cycled through the colors of the chakras until settling into a bright yellow.

"Slowly open your eyes."

Sarah's eyes fluttered open and widened as she saw the glowing orb in her hands.

"Wow," Sarah breathed.

Zazzie smiled.

"This is your core energy. It's different for everyone, and not everyone can manifest it in this way."

Sarah slowly spread her hands apart. The single orb separated into two, her right hand glowed bright blue, and her left a fiery red.

"This is so cool!"

Zazzie nodded.

"Just be careful. Explore, but don't use your energies just yet. Can you tell me what you feel or see? Does the room seem different in any way?"

Sarah slowly turned her head, taking everything in.

"Everything has its own color. You are a rainbow, but your colors are faded like they are weakened somehow."

Zazzie focused on building up walls against Sarah's intrusion.

"First rule of Aura society. It's rude to read people's Auras without permission."

Sarah's light dimmed, and she hung her head.

"Sorry."

"No worries, you are still new to this. Can you still see my energy?"

Sarah looked up, her brow creased in concentration. Zazzie felt the waves of the attempted intrusion, but was confident her walls would hold.

"It's like I can feel there is energy there, but I can't make out exactly what is there. It's like a wall."

"Exactly. Once you master finding and connecting with energies, I will show you how to block them, as well. Now, that's all we have time for today. I want you to practice connecting with your core energy in a safe space, of course. While showering or taking a bath will help shield your energy from others."

"Okay," Sarah said and stood.

Zazzie winced as Sarah collapsed on top of her.

"I forgot to warn you to be careful after practicing. You might not feel how draining it is initially, but once you can do so without so much effort, you won't need to worry about the weakness that follows."

Sarah rolled over onto her back and snorted.

"Great, so it's just like connecting with your inner beast. I thought I was done with this feeling," she grumbled.

Zazzie reached for her bag and pulled out a bottle of water and a granola bar.

"Take a few minutes, and you should be okay to make it home."

Sarah took the provisions offered and smiled.

"Thank you," she added as she left.

Zazzie lingered in the space. She couldn't believe just yesterday she had been ecstatic to get home and spend time with Hendrex, and now she could barely face him. There was so much she wanted to say to him, and yet she just couldn't. So here she was, avoiding going home. She couldn't do this forever; she couldn't let this be how things ended between them. She pushed herself off the floor and headed home.

When she arrived, all the lights were off, and Hendrex was asleep on the couch. With a sigh, she made her way to her empty bedroom, climbing into the pile of pillows and soft blankets. She was supposed to be the Zenith. He was supposed to be with her on her journey. Had the ancestors lied to her? Had they shown her what she wanted to get her to do their bidding? That didn't make any sense. A lot of what they had shown her was nothing she would ever wish for, so why would they lie about Hendrex? She fell into a fitful sleep, replaying the ancestor message over and over in her brain. She had been chosen. She was the Zenith. She was the vehicle for her people's future. The shepherd of the children, the guiding star, and yet, she felt so incredibly lost.

Overworked

Hendrex stood atop the mountain overlooking the city of Langsmith. The city was on fire. Plumes of smoke mingled with bright red shocks of flame. Nearly every building was set aflame. There was a soft rustle behind him. He turned from the carnage below. Zazzie approached, her skin glowing so brightly he had to shield his eyes to look at her. Her deep brown eyes were completely blighted by deep black, not an ounce of white shown in them. She hovered above the ground, her long skirts dragging through the soft dirt of the clearing. Her locs flowed around her head as if they had a mind of their own. She reached out to him with one hand, the other hand resting on her exposed belly. Her extended belly, full of the promise of life.

Hendrex took her hand. Heat shot through him. Like a searing brand of love and light just before he sank into the earth. Swallowed whole by the mountain, the soil and rock surrounding him, blocking out her light, choking him as his mouth and lungs filled with earth. The rocks pressed into his body, squeezing the life out of him as it pulled him farther into its depths.

Suddenly, he could move his feet, then his legs, and he fell. Landing with a hard thud on more jagged stones.

He coughed, his whole body spasming as it cleared the soil away to gasp for air. Zazzie appeared again, this time gliding away from him and toward a large boulder, pulsing from the inside with an energy so intense it racked over Hendrex like hot ashes blown from the fires below.

He shook his head. More soil fell from his ears, revealing a soft humming. It was low and pulsating like the light, a heartbeat. Zazzie touched the stone with her palm. The light drained from her body and into the massive boulder. The humming intensified; the pulsing increased until it reached a fever pitch. Strobing beams of light broke the surface. The rock cracked like an egg, revealing the source of the lights. It wasn't alive. It was a piece of technology far beyond even what the humans had created. The rock fell away, revealing a shining metal egg. With a hiss of hydraulics, a door slowly split the smooth ovoid shape. Hendrex crawled forward, curiosity-fueling his movements.

Inside, there was a control panel of sorts and what looked like two seats. It was a ship. A hologram of a strange figure appeared. The words were garbled and incomprehensible, but Zazzie seemed to understand exactly what the creature said. She spread her legs wide, squatting in the dirt. A sweat broke out over her brow. She grunted and strained, then screamed—a rush of fluids leaked from beneath her skirts.

Hendrex crawled closer, still unable to move his wrecked body as much as he would have liked. Zazzie reached into her skirt, and with one final scream, she fell onto her back. In her arms, she held three babies, triplets. Their bodies were covered in thick white goo. Zazzie laughed and cried, kissing the tops of their small heads. Then she carefully placed one child inside of the egg ship.

"Your destiny awaits—our hope for the future. I

return you home, my son, and anxiously await your return.

Hendrex watched on in horror as the doors closed on his child.

Waking in a cold sweat, Hendrex reached for Zarovia. His hand met nothing but a soft cushion. With a sigh, he stared at the ceiling.

"It was all a dream. Just a dream," he muttered to himself before rolling off the couch and stretching.

Zazzie was already gone. She'd been avoiding him the last few days, and this was the third time he'd had this crazy dream this week. It had to be a manifestation of his fear of losing Zazzie for good. Things had been tense between them for days, but she hadn't kicked him out yet, so there was that.

Zazzie had been spending long hours at work, and now that it was finally the weekend, he had hoped they would eventually have the talk they desperately needed to have. Instead, she had disappeared into the commercial part of her house. Hendrex didn't like the idea of strangers being so close to her personal space. It wasn't safe, especially now with the Vampires acting like rabid fools. It would be a struggle, but he would have to convince her to move once he was in a position to support her the way he should. However, it wasn't the time to bring up his issues with her side work, especially after the fiasco with Jasmine and their non-argument after.

He was wiping down the counters in the kitchen when his phone buzzed. It wasn't Mack, as he expected. Mack was the only person who called him on his phone. Few others had his number, or had any reason to call him otherwise. Even the other members of their little association didn't bother calling him directly. They were content to send missives through his brother.

Hendrex almost didn't answer as the number came up as private. If the person was blocking their number, then it probably wasn't someone he wanted to hear from to begin with. Still, he pressed the button out of habit.

"Hello?"

"Dre. My man. You got a minute."

Hendrex smiled. It was Icarus.

"Yeah, what's up?"

"I've got a bit of a situation I need your help with."

Hendrex bit back a groan. He could only imagine what kind of trouble Icarus had gotten himself into and prayed it had nothing to do with Jasmine. As it was, Hendrex would need to be careful to avoid being anywhere unchaperoned with her. Of course, that wasn't the only thing Hendrex would be reluctant to help him with.

It was one thing if this was a friendly call. It was another if this was Council business. Hendrex was okay with mentoring him, but it only made it harder for Hendrex to let go of what happened with the previous Council. He could advise, but to be honest, he wasn't sure how much help he truly was. The Council was an entirely different entity now.

He would do this one last thing for Icarus, but after that, he would need to focus on getting his own crap together. Still, Icarus was a friend, and Hendrex didn't have enough of those to be so cavalier about it.

"What do you need?"

"I can't really talk about it over the phone. Can you meet me at Fowler Park? It's next to the fairgrounds."

Hendrex glanced around the room as if there was anything there to give him an excuse to back out. There wasn't, and Hendrex had nothing else on his agenda for the day.

"Yeah, man, give me thirty minutes," he said.

Icarus sighed with relief.

"Thanks, man, I owe you one for sure."

Hendrex hung up the phone, shaking his head. He finished wiping down the counters before going into the bedroom to change clothes. He hoped Icarus was being dramatic and whatever he needed help with was something small. Then again, Icarus had proved quite capable of handling himself, and Fowler Park was smack in the middle of Rogue Vampire territory.

Hendrex pulled out his phone again and texted Mack.

H: Hey, bro. I'm headed to Fowler Park.

Mack responded almost immediately.

M: What the fuck for?

H: Not sure, but keep your phone on you just in case I need some backup.

M: Fuck that. I'll meet you there.

Hendrex didn't know whether to be relieved or anxious about his brother's sudden willingness to come running.

H: Like I said, not sure that's needed.

M: Boo fucking hoo, bro. Fowler Park is not safe to just be traipsing around unprepared. You ain't changing my mind. You at Zazzie's? I'll come to pick you up.

Hendrex knew his brother seriously would not let it drop, and he didn't want to bother Zazzie by asking to borrow her car, so he relented.

H: Yeah, I'm at Zazzie's. See you in a bit.

Mack was already parked out front when Hendrex got to the door.

"You armed?" Mack called from the open window of his busted SUV.

"Keep your voice down, Zazzie's neighbors are nosy, and I don't want them to call the cops 'cause two black men outside yelled about being armed," Hendrex chastised his brother.

Mack laughed.

"We'll be long gone before any cops show up. They'll be too busy cleaning up the mess from last night."

Hendrex slid into the passenger seat.

"What mess?"

"Nothing specific, at least, not for us to be concerned with."

Hendrex tried to put the seatbelt on, but it got stuck just before it reached the buckle. The more Hendrex pulled, the shorter it got until he gave it a final tug, and the seatbelt fell from its housing.

"When are you going to upgrade this piece of shit? You aren't undercover anymore."

Mack shook his head and reached in the backseat before tossing Hendrex a bungee cord.

"This from the man riding his girl's whip around town. Don't talk shit, just get in."

"Seriously! What the fuck am I supposed to do with this? This thing is a death trap. I'm surprised Disrayan lets you keep this thing."

"Again, you can talk when you aren't living off your girl."

Mack pulled away from Zazzie's house just as an older woman in a white sedan parked in front of the business entrance of Zazzie's place. Hendrex couldn't help himself from checking the woman out. He read her energy and felt something was off, but Mack was already turning around the corner. Zarovia could handle herself. Besides, anyone coming to Zazzie was bound to be off in some way; otherwise, they wouldn't be frequenting her shop. Another reason Hendrex was uneasy about her chosen side profession.

"So, what's going down at Fowler Park?" Mack asked.

"I told you, I don't know exactly. Just got a call from Icarus asking to come by."

"Say less," Mack said before pressing his foot to the floor.

Mack made the twenty-minute drive to Fowler Park in ten. The park was seemingly deserted; the only movement was the breeze dancing through the treetops and the occasional bird. Hendrex got out of the car, but Mack stayed behind.

"You coming?"

Mack shook his head. "I'll come if there's a reason to. You meet up with Icarus, I'll hang back in case we need to call for more reinforcements."

***

Drawing the black velvet curtain closed over the door to the rest of her house, Zazzie officially started her business hours. She had three readings that afternoon, followed by a bachelorette party in the evening. Zazzie rarely did readings outside of a controlled environment, but the changes to her life goals necessitated the extra funds. She hadn't discussed it with anyone yet, but she saw a need in the handling of the youth and those who had their energies awakened by the blast. They needed a school, and while the Aura had some wealth in the human world, most of it was being used to help the refugees get on their feet. It would take years before anyone got around to starting an official education program, and it would be at a detriment to the Aura.

So evidenced by the madness that came into her office that week. Daphne and Sarah had only been the start. The very next day an Aura boy was suspended for harming a human student. It had been an accident. His heightened emotions from being bullied all day had triggered a release of energy so big she'd felt it on the other side of campus. At least, no one had been there to witness the incident, and the human boy thought the kid had shoved him hard enough to send him halfway across a room and into several desks.

Her after-school class had grown from three to fifteen in less than a week. She couldn't blame the kids. They had enough to deal with just with school and puberty, add to that additional Aura training and the threat of Vampire retaliation. It was a wonder the entire district wasn't up in flames. The conference room wasn't big enough to fit the students anymore, so they had moved to the cafeteria. It wasn't ideal, and soon, they would need much more space, both indoor and outdoor. So here she was, pushing her limits and her comfort zone to hopefully save enough to cover the already growing costs of her new program.

The tinkling of the bell on her storefront door signaled the arrival of her first appointment. A middle-aged woman dressed in a flowing tie dye maxi dress floated into her space. Zazzie made her way to the front with a bright smile on her face.

"Sheila, please take a moment to look around. I am almost set for your reading today."

Sheila was a regular. She came in monthly, bought a few crystals, and was typically satisfied with a basic tarot reading for whatever plagued her most that month. Which alternated between if her son's latest girlfriend would be the one or if her health would take a turn for the worst. Thankfully, Sheila was satisfied with the answers Zazzie provided. Yet this afternoon, Sheila's energy seemed off, and that wasn't a good sign.

To be truthful, the tarot was mostly for show. Zazzie relied on her empathic energy to read people and provide the more in-depth analysis she had become known for. She stood just out of sight, studying Sheila from a safe distance. She followed the trail of troubling energy to the center of the woman's chest. Working with people's emotions often coincided with being able to recognize the body's physical cues of emotion.

Sheila's breathing was shallow and slightly labored. Her chest had a stuttered cadence to its rise and fall. She rested a little too much on the displays as she made her way around the room. Closing her eyes, Zazzie envisioned the internal workings of the human body. Enora might be known for her knowledge of anatomy as a medical examiner, but many forgot that Zazzie had completed some of the same coursework with her. Zeroing in on the problem, Zazzie's own heart rate slowed, her consciousness drifted above, her body energy danced in a rainbow of colors around the room exuding from every space. The sickly green surrounding Sheila concentrated near her heart and lungs before fading into a yellowish red.

Zazzie forced herself back into her corporeal form, her eyes flashing open just in time to see Sheila's eyes roll back into her head before she crumpled to the floor. Zazzie rushed over, pulling her phone out of her pocket as she dialed for help. Sheila's eyes fluttered open in the middle of Zazzie providing the dispatcher with her address. Placing a hand on Sheila's chest, she kept the woman from sitting up too quickly. She exuded a calming energy to keep Sheila from panicking and possibly making the situation worse before the paramedics could arrive.

By the time they arrived and got Sheila loaded into the back of the ambulance, Zazzie was exhausted. This was too much excitement for one day. With Sheila in good hands, Zazzie went back inside to begin clearing the space for her next appointment. Any other day, she would call and reschedule, but the needs of the teens were much greater than her need for rest.

She did her usual routine of cleansing the negative energy from her work space before sitting for a little restorative meditation in the last ten minutes before her next appointment was supposed to arrive. Settling onto her mat, she folded her legs beneath her body, the tension in her ankles a distraction and a centering force all at once. Taking a deep breath, she settled into herself, blocking out everything but the glowing center of her energy.

The normally bright pulsating orb was dimmer and slower, a sure sign that she was overtaxing her abilities. She changed the rhythm of her breathing, two short intakes through her mouth and one long exhale out the nose, ramping up her body, allowing herself to sink deeper and deeper into herself, almost to the point of no return.

Zazzie had learned at a very young age that connecting and communing with the deepest parts of oneself was more restorative than any perfume laden bath or deep tissue massage. Knowing who you were at your very core helped you cope with almost anything the universe could throw your way. After drawing as much positive energy as she could into her core, she allowed consciousness to slowly float back to the surface. There was no real way of judging how long she had been within herself, but from years of practice, she had learned to pull herself out between 10-30 minutes.

You need rest!

Zazzie's brain tried to force itself into the conversation with her body. She held her breath, forcing herself to return to the world slowly despite the intrusion of her mind.

You need rest!

Zazzie's womb spoke to her now. She released the breath she held and let her eyes flutter open. She felt better, but not nearly as recharged as she had hoped. It wasn't her style to ignore the plea of her inner self, but for the children she was willing to sacrifice just a bit more. The soft jingle of her shop door announced her next client. Pushing herself off the floor, Zazzie made her way back into the storefront.

The smile she normally offered her customers fell immediately at the sight of the redheaded Vampiress perusing her wares.

"I'm sorry, I am only open for appointments at the moment."

Molly looked up and smiled, not bothering to hide her razor-sharp fangs.

"I have an opportunity I wish to discuss with you."

Zazzie crossed her arms over her chest and shook her head. Not that she had anything against Molly, she was just so tired she couldn't add anything extra to her plate, and that included curious Vampires. No matter how nice they were.

"Can we talk about it later? I have a customer arriving soon and now will have to cleanse this space all over again," she said, hoping Molly didn't detect the edge of annoyance in her voice.

It really wasn't the woman's fault Zazzie was in such a bad mood.

Molly's eyes squinted as she studied Zazzie before her bright smile returned.

"No problem, I will wait for your call, and you know where to find me if you would rather chat in person."

Molly practically bounced out of the store, nearly knocking over Zazzie's actual customer who was poised reaching for the door handle as Molly flung the door open. Zazzie fixed her face into a smile for her customer and guided her inside.

"Sorry about that," she said.

The customer smiled and started rambling away about the reason for her appointment.

***

The last person Sarah expected to hear from that weekend was Daphne. Sure, they had been hanging out a bit more in school, but not so much outside of it. Still, when Sequoia had overheard Sarah on the phone with Daphne, her look of excitement was enough to have Sarah agreeing to meet Daphne at the mall.

"Look at you, making friends, going to the mall!" Sequoia gushed.

"Please, Coy. It's not that big of a deal."

"What's not that big of a deal?" Tyr asked, coming into the cabin.

"Sarah is going with a friend to the mall," Coy said

Tyr smiled briefly before his smile dropped.

"A friend or a boyfriend?" he asked.

"Daphne Orion," Sequoia clarified for her.

"Oh, that's cool, I guess, but remember to be back before the curfew."

Sequoia rolled her eyes at Tyr's back as he headed farther into the cabin. Coy went over to her purse and pulled out her wallet.

"Here's my card. Don't go crazy with it, but have fun, okay?" she said.

Sarah nodded and accepted the card. She had no intention of using it, but didn't want to reject Coy's kind offer. Sarah was doing her best to accept Coy's motherly gestures for what they were. A sign of her affection. It wasn't easy for Sarah to accept it because of her past, but she was done letting her past rule her life.

"Thanks, Coy. I promise to be back by curfew."

Sarah met Daphne in front of the local ice cream shop.

"You don't actually plan to go to the mall, do you?" Sarah said, noting Daphne's all black attire.

"No, but I know Shifters can smell a lie a mile away, and I didn't want to get you in trouble," she said.

"So, what do you think we're doing today?"

"Just going for a casual stroll," Daphne replied.

"Fine, whatever, but if we happen across Vampires, we are not engaging, you hear me? I'm not ruining my clothes to save your ass this time."

"I don't need saving!"

"Ugh, let's not start this again."

"Fine, let's go." Daphne trailed off in a random direction, and Sarah reluctantly followed.

"You know, this is stupid, right? I've lived my whole life on my own, fighting for my life, and even I don't go looking for fights," Sarah said.

"I'm not looking for a fight, I'm just finishing the one they started," Daphne said.

Sarah grabbed her arm and stopped her.

"Are you out of your mind? Do you want to end up in a cage again? Why can't you just stop for a second and think about how lucky you are to have a second chance at being normal?"

"Normal! How can I be normal? Everyone knows what happened to me. Poor Daphne, she was duped by a human boy, poor Daphne, she was kidnapped by Vampires, poor Daphne, she must be so messed up from her ordeal!"

"Fuck them! All that matters is what you think of yourself."

"Easy for you to say, you've never cared what others think," Daphne said.

"It wasn't that I didn't care, it was that I learned not to. You made an honest mistake, and there are people like me and Keenan who couldn't care less about what happened."

Daphne's anger evaporated, and a smile lit her face.

"You really think Keenan cares?"

Sarah resisted the urge to slap the girl.

"Of course, I care, Daph," Keenan appeared from around the corner.

"How long have you been there?"

"I've been following you two since the ice cream shop." He walked up to Daphne and pulled her into a hug.

"Don't worry about those goons. I've got you, Daph. If anyone gives you shit, just let me know, and I'll set them straight."

"Ugh, can we get off the street? Maybe actually go to the mall?"

"Who goes to the mall?" Keenan scowled.

"I don't know, but that's what I told Tyr, and unless y'all want to get on the bad side of the Alpha Shifter in town, we better, at least, make it a stop on this little tour."

Keenan winced, and Daphne bit her lip.

"Alright, but let's go grab some ice cream first."

"Ice cream, really?"

Keenan smiled.

"Why did you think I was at the shop, to see you two delinquents?"

Daphne and Sarah both rolled their eyes.

"Alright, ice cream first, then the mall."

✳✳✳

Mack watched as Hendrex walked farther into the park. For all the smarts his brother had, this was one of the stupidest things he could ever remember him doing. Well, this and not telling Zazzie how he felt sooner. He'd meant to ask his brother how things were going with her, but Hendrex's foul mood made it obvious things weren't going well.

Mack scanned the area for energies, but it was no use. The whole space reeked with negative energy, both fresh and residual. There was no telling where the danger lurked in the calm of the empty park.

His phone buzzed in his pocket, and he pulled it out.

H: No sign of Icarus yet.

Mack scowled. He didn't like this one bit. It reeked of a set up.

M: It's not too late to get back in the car and demand you meet somewhere else.

Mack looked up to see Hendrex looking back at him from across the park. Hendrex shook his head in the negative and continued on. Mack dialed Shane's number, and the Vampire answered almost immediately.

"Hey, man. What's up?"

"I'm at Fowler Park with my brother. Just wanted to let someone know where we were in case things went south."

"Fowler Park? You asking for a fight? Hendrex didn't strike me as the type to go out looking for trouble."

Mack snorted.

"I know I get the bad twin wrap, but Hendrex is no saint. Anyway, this is just a precaution."

"Alright, I'll keep my phone on me, just in case. We can get there in about thirty minutes if need be."

"Thanks, man," Mack said and hung up.

He contemplated texting Jaq about the situation, but Jaq would insist on showing up and then there would definitely be a fight. With how things had gone down, any public appearance by Jaq was a fight on sight for any Vampire in the area. It didn't matter that he wasn't the one who actually killed Maximus, Jaq was arguably an easier target than Molly who had actually killed the man and most of the Vampires involved in the attack on the Aura.

Tyr was also an option to call. He surely had people on patrol that could jump in to help, but things with the Shifters were tense after the death of Maximus. Tyr was on their side, but that didn't mean the rest of the Shifters in his pack would drop everything to help them out. The Shifters were more likely to stand by and watch, rather than offer any real help. Not all Shifters were as open to the plight of the Aura as Tyr. Years of being on the sidelines had taught them not to take sides in conflicts that didn't directly involve them.

The help Tyr had offered so far was enough to have him removed from his position as Alpha of the Langsmith Pack if anyone caught wind of just how much he had helped in the past. No, Mack wouldn't risk endangering Tyr's status over something like this. He looked up again. Hendrex was almost out of sight. Cursing, he got out of the car and tucked a pistol into his pants. Bullets wouldn't do much but slow down a Vampire for a second or two, but that sometimes made the difference needed to get away safely.

Mack started after his brother, hanging back just enough not to spook Icarus or whoever waited for Hendrex to arrive. There was movement behind one of the larger trees. Mack's hand immediately went to his pistol, but relaxed when Icarus appeared with three young teens.

At least, it really had been Icarus who requested this shady meeting in the park. That didn't mean everything was on the up and up. Mack studied the group; they were scanning the area in an aggressive manner, but they directed none of their aggression toward Hendrex. Mack relaxed a little, knowing it hadn't been an outright set up.

***

Hendrex froze when Icarus appeared. His energy felt off, not nervous or angry, but definitely not calm either. Icarus looked around before approaching Hendrex.

"I'm glad you could make it."

Hendrex was relieved things didn't appear to be desperately wrong, but he wasn't a fan of this meeting place or the secretive nature of Icarus's call. The Ruling Council had enough on their plate that a clandestine meeting with one of the Ruling Council was more than suspect. Not to mention, the group of teen boys that followed him.

"What's going on?"

Hendrex eyed the group of teens with Icarus. He recognized them as a few of the kids living at the Factory. All of them were Aura.

"Sorry to have to do this in such an awful place, but we needed to talk where other Aura wouldn't overhear."

That peaked Hendrex's interest and unease.

"Okay?"

"We want to take classes with Ms. Monoceros, but our parents won't allow it. They think she will taint us," one teen spoke.

"So, what do you want me to do?"

"Ms. Monoceros has her classes at the Factory. We won't be able to train there without our parents and Ms. Hyperion finding out."

"What does this have to do with Ms. Hyperion?"

The boys exchanged looks.

"She doesn't believe in blending human and Aura education, and frankly, she scares us. When we mentioned being interested in the class, her eyes."

One boy nudged the boy who was talking, and he shut up.

"That doesn't explain my involvement."

"Well, we can't train with Ms. Monoceros, and we

aren't comfortable with The Resistance. We were hoping you could teach us?"

Hendrex eyed Icarus. There had to be more to the story than this, but for now, he was willing to let it slide. The sooner they figured this out, the sooner they could leave this dangerous place.

"Is this an official Council ask? I thought the Council was behind Zarovia's school. Even Ms. Hyperion?"

Icarus rolled his eyes.

"Let's just say it wasn't a unanimous agreement and more that she chose to honor the decision made by the previous Ruling Council."

Hendrex shook his head. There shouldn't already be this much division in the Council. Then again, pretending there wasn't any in the last Council was most likely what led to the fall of Ceres to begin with. They had all been too afraid of tarnishing their larger-than-life reputations than the actual plight of the people.

"You know acting outside of the Council is what got us here in the first place," he chastised Icarus.

"I know, but in this, I don't see any other way. They have a valid point, and the Council won't want to discuss the same topic again. Especially now."

Hendrex didn't need to elaborate on the "especially now". Hendrex knew exactly what it meant. Jasmine Hyperion was taking out her anger on Zazzie through the school issue. It wasn't fair, and Hendrex had a feeling it was more his fault than anything Zazzie had done. He'd been avoiding Jasmine just as much as Zarovia had been avoiding him.

"Alright, alright. I will figure out a solution. I promise. Was there anything else?"

The boys looked between themselves before the most vocal of them shook their head.

"No, that was it."

Hendrex studied the boys. Their energy was chaotic. They were lying to him. There was more, but Hendrex was picking up on more concerning energies at the moment.

"We need to go," Icarus said.

"It's too late," Hendrex said, gathering his energy to cast at the fast-approaching group of Rogue Vampires.

Hendrex could tell they were Rogues because their energy held an extra tinge of death. The fear and pain of their victims lingered on them. There was no bagged blood for them. They preferred drinking from the source, and the stench of fear it brought, they wore like a badge of honor.

If his count was correct, there were six Vampires coming straight for them from behind. Two he could handle easily, with the help of Icarus another two would be covered, but that left two more to deal with. His best chance was to create a force field and hold them off until he could reach Mack for back up.

Hendrex kept them at bay long enough for the group of boys to scatter. He reached out to Mack, thankful Mack wasn't still waiting in the car but was almost right behind them.

"I'll be back once I make sure these idiot kids don't get caught," Mack shouted before going after the boys. At least, they would be safe, but that didn't solve Hendrex's immediate problem. Icarus stayed behind to fight. Hendrex dropped his shield in time to refocus his energy into his hands. Shooting beams of energy straight at the Vampire's hearts. It wouldn't kill them unless they were newly turned. Otherwise, it would knock them out long enough for Mack and the boys to make a clean get away. Hendrex got three before the others got smart and dodged his attacks. Thankfully, Icarus was there as back up; his energy wasn't as strong, but it was enough to stun the rest of them.

"Come on, let's go!"

Hendrex started back toward Mack's car, but Icarus grabbed his arm and dragged him in the opposite direction. He would have tried to move Icarus in a different direction if he hadn't belatedly picked up on ten more Vampire energies in that direction. Fear spiked in Hendrex's heart as he realized they were surrounded. It seemed the boys and Mack had slipped through before the Vampires had closed off all avenues of escape.

Icarus and Hendrex stood back-to-back as they faced off with the encroaching Vampire hoard.

***

Brody pulled up to Fowler Park and checked his watch. He'd dealt with Rogues in the past, and they were never on a gentlemen's schedule. It was annoying, and he knew they wouldn't have kept him waiting this long if he were anything more than Merwin's errand boy.

"How did I get here?" he muttered.

He knew exactly how he had gotten there—arrogance, ego, greed, a fear of death. Becoming a Vampire was supposed to have given him a better life. He'd left his entire family back in Oracle, a lovely little family, a nice little farm. He could have lived a long and boring life with his pretty but shallow wife and their two kids, but he hadn't been happy. He hadn't been satisfied with the 2.5 kids and picket fence, so when danger came knocking, he'd made a deal with the devil. He'd traded his family for a life of gilded servitude.

A gaggle of humans running by his nondescript black sedan brought his attention back to reality.

"What the hell!"

He couldn't see anything from his parking spot, so he got out of the car. Immediately, he felt it, the familiar zip of electricity in the air like the aftermath of a lightning strike. He shook his head. Whatever was happening here, it couldn't be good. He pulled out his phone. His Rogue contact had sent him a message about showing his worth as a leader.

The sounds of battle reached his sensitive ears, the steady thud of physical blows and groans of pain. He should have gotten back in his car, but the next swarm of Vampires speeding across his path gave him pause. What in the world was going on here? An outright attack in broad daylight? Brody wanted no part in this egregious miscalculation, but he also didn't dare report back to Merwin emptyhanded.

Maximus had loved to throw his weight around, but Brody had been confident of his standing with the man. Merwin was much more ruthless and calculating. Brody shivered at the thought of what punishment he would endure if he screwed this up. So, he pressed onward, following the Vampire hoard to the scene of which Brody had never witnessed before. Vampires, Shifters, and more magic users than Brody had ever seen in the wild.

Brody stood entranced by the spectacle of it all. Doing his own calculations, Langsmith had a much larger population of the coveted magic users than previously thought, and much more powerful ones at that. His fangs descended. If he could get his hands on one of them, maybe he too could strike out on his own. He'd be more powerful than the entire Vampire Council if he got his hands on one of the two magic users standing in the middle of the chaos. His greed was quickly squashed by his own self-preservation skills. A blue orb whizzed by his head; the heat singed the tips of his ears.

He turned to see a young Aura female a few feet away, preparing to wing another orb at him. He would never gain power as a dead man, well, a truly dead man. He used his Vampire speed to escape back to his car. When he looked back toward the park, he expected to see the flashing glow of magic being used in great magnitude, but he saw nothing. Something or someone concealed the fight.

Shaking his head, he sent a text back to his contact.

"If you survive this fiasco, you better have something to provide the buyer."

With that, he drove away. There was no reason to let himself get caught up in yet another fiasco here in Langsmith.

***

Hendrex was gone when Zazzie finally closed her shop for the day. Other than the visit from Molly, the rest of her schedule had gone as planned. Yet, instead of feeling relaxed that her work day was over, she had been tensely awaiting her confrontation with Hendrex, but he hadn't even stuck around for it. She wanted to be angry, but she could tell that something was off. The energy in the air felt very much like the day Ceres had fallen. An ominous energy lingered in the air, waiting to latch on to its unsuspecting victims. Zazzie checked her phone but there was no message from Hendrex, which was weird. He was typically very communicative about his whereabouts, even if they were avoiding each other. It was a precaution they both took during these troubling times.

It has begun.

The whisper came out of thin air and made Zazzie jump. Her house was warded, there shouldn't be any wayward spirits, but with how off she'd felt lately, there was a small chance she had made a misstep in her routine while closing her shop.

119

Zenith. It has begun.

That was definitely not a wayward spirit, and that could only mean— Zazzie's blood ran cold. "No!"

She was just about to dial his number when her phone buzzed with a text in her friends' group.

Farrah: 911 Fowler Park

Disrayan: Already on my way. Enora, you better stay your pregnant ass home!

Enora: Jaq already sent people to protect me. I'll be prepping a triage area. This sounds bad.

Farrah: Zazzie? You still working?

Zazzie stopped zoning out and focused her frantic energy into her fingers to type out a reply.

Z: I'm on my way now.

Farrah: Don't over work yourself. Go help Enora.

Disrayan: I'm here. Shit, we need all hands-on deck. Enora still stay your ass at home.

Keys already in hand, Zazzie took off toward her car. It was turning out to be a banner day for emotional upheaval. She hopped in the car, her palms sweaty and slick on the leather-covered steering wheel. She kept herself only ten miles per hour over the speed limit as she anxiously headed toward Fowler Park.

Her heart nearly stopped when she parked next to Disrayan's car. It was like the night the Vampires attacked the gate to Ceres. Vampires, Shifters, and Aura. It was chaos, it was bloody, it was all-out war. There was no time for containment. Already, there were stunned and frightened humans gawking at the spectacle of impossibility in front of them.

In the center of it all stood Hendrex and Icarus. She could see their energies waning from the near constant battle they faced. She wanted to help them, but she knew she wasn't strong enough. Especially, after this morning. Her best effort would be in trying to contain the fight enough to avoid the human authorities becoming involved.

It is time!

She knew what to do. This was the start of her journey as Zenith. She had to give her all for her people, that was her destiny. Zazzie didn't dare close her eyes as she focused on her energy. Drawing from her core, she singled out the out-of-place humans, manipulating them into leaving. The few who had pulled out their phones, she had them drop them as they ran. The phones could be collected and scrubbed later. For now, she did her best to create what was in human terms, a glamour spell. She couldn't cover everything, but she could, at least, replace bolts of energy with perceived bullets and projectiles from this angle of the fight. It was the best she could do with her limited reserves and still keep enough to protect herself from falling victim to the blood bath in front of her.

A few of the Aura noticed what she was doing and joined in creating a secure glamour over the entire battle scene before them. That took some of the stress off Zazzie as she could reduce her glamour to a more manageable area and draw less from her core energy. As long as the battle didn't go on for more than an hour.

The fight seemed to go on for ages. Her eyes tracking the movement around her, she spotted Mack cradling a limp Disrayan in his arms, and Zazzie nearly lost her hold on her glamour. It was a good thing she hadn't. There were already several spectators lined up behind her and Sarah came bursting through the crowd. Her energy flowed out in a massive wave, knocking over any and every one in her path. Sarah took Disrayan from Mack, and with a nod of understanding, she took off carrying Disrayan out of harm's way.

Zazzie paused to wipe the sweat from her brow. Her

arms were getting heavy and her energy was depleting quicker now as exhaustion took its toll.

Once Disrayan was safely outside of the fighting, Mack turned back to the mob and unleashed an energy so dark and vicious even Zazzie had a hard time believing her eyes. She'd known Mack's energy was different, but she hadn't realized just how different. There was nothing light or natural about what emanated from him. As if that wasn't enough, Molly had arrived. The redhead stood out even amongst the motley crew of creatures. Her curls bounced effortlessly as if she were strutting through a scenic park in a shampoo commercial. It was disconcerting considering the lightness of her step was more to avoid the remains of those who fell dead at her feet. It wasn't the massive bubble of death she used to protect the Aura. At first, it seemed to be restricted to just a few feet around her but it was enough to send more of the Vampires into retreat.

Molly made her way to the center of the group and placed a hand on Hendrex's shoulder. Zazzie hated how he smiled down at Molly, as if she were the answer to all his prayers. He had never looked at Zazzie in that way. The sudden streak of jealousy shook Zazzie's control of her energy. Even knowing Molly was most definitely not interested and most definitely spoken for, didn't ease the gnawing in her gut. Zarovia Monoceros was not the jealous type. Hell, she'd even been in a few polyamorous entanglements in her life. Yet, here she was more concerned about the way Hendrex smiled at another woman than focusing on keeping the human authorities from coming across a massive battle between Supernaturals in the middle of the city in broad daylight.

One of the Aura holding the glamour suddenly collapsed, and the battle in her section quickly spilled beyond the bounds of her position. Other Aura scrambled to cover the newly exposed segment, but their time was up. Sirens screamed in the distance, and they were getting closer. Molly must have heard them too because she looked up, the whites of her eyes glowing so bright they obscured her irises. Her shroud of death slowly expanded as it had before, this time, instead of only destroying their attackers, her energy turned the fallen into dust as well.

"Shit!" Zazzie couldn't help the curse that slipped out of her mouth.

This was not going to be good. No matter how the battles between Rogue Vampires and the other Supernaturals went. A proper burial was always allowed for the fallen. Molly had just set a precedent that neither side would be agreeable to. Even in war, there was some sense of decorum. There was no time to go over just how egregious her act was. The sirens were too close. Zazzie dropped her glamour and ran forward, straight to Hendrex. He caught her in his arms and kissed her with a desperation and passion that nearly had her clawing at his clothes in the middle of all the chaos.

"We have to go!" The voice of Icarus broke the spell of lust around them.

Hendrex took off toward the first line of trees with Zazzie in his arms. The cops were too close for them to try to escape by car. Her carried her as if she weighed next to nothing. Hendrex was strong, but not that strong. His adrenaline the most likely culprit in keeping his body from crumpling in an exhausted heap. There was no telling who was friend or foe as the need to escape the custody of human authorities became prime on everyone's agenda.

Zazzie was forced to close her eyes as branches, thick and thin, slapped against her as they ran deeper into the woods. She had no way of knowing where they were going, but as long as she was with Hendrex, she knew she was safe. At least, physically.

Doors Open

Merwin listened to Brody's report on Langsmith and the Rogue's blatant disrespect of Vampire law. His grip on the phone tightened with each new act of aggression and egregious disrespect the toad of a man rattled off. The device creaked and groaned, very near its breaking point. His anger was justified but not the threads of shock running through his veins. The perpetrators were Rogues; their flouting of Vampire law was to be expected. In most cases, these things were easily handled with a few dollars or favors to the human authorities, but this was entirely too public to explain away. The Protectorate would surely move in on Langsmith, and his supply chain to the most powerful magic users left in the world would cease to exist.

"Gather the Council, tell them I have appointed you as temporary liaison," he said, cutting off Brody's ambling.

"Temporary? Our deal was that if I could establish a new funnel, I would be given the position," Brody said.

Merwin laughed.

"Those were the terms you offered. I never accepted. Now, do as your told, get the Council in order and make sure my niece doesn't stick her pretty little head where it doesn't belong. I don't want her bad attitude becoming public knowledge and ruining my chances at marrying her off."

Merwin hung up before Brody could reply.

Maximus was a fool if he thought Brody had any real merit to him. Brody was a clout chaser, plain and simple. Easily manipulated and not at all trustworthy. The situation in Langsmith wasn't ideal, but it was still salvageable. Even if Merwin had to send an army there, he would regain control of the magic population there.

A knock on the office door signaled Merwin's guest. He stood and straightened his clothing before answering.

"You may enter," he said.

"Good evening, sir." Cain said, coming into the study.

Cain had turned out to be quite the disappointment. Despite his fairly good looks and strong abilities, he somehow let several Alulpo mates slip out of his grasp. If he hadn't publicly embarrassed himself over the last Alulpo, Merwin may have considered him as a possible mate for Carrie. She could use someone with a firm hand, but now he wasn't quite sure Cain fit that bill. Either way, he could still be useful.

"I need you to go to Langsmith."

Cain scoffed, "Langsmith, seriously? Is this my punishment for not winning the Alulpo woman?"

Merwin cut his eyes at Cain.

"The beating you received wasn't punishment enough?"

Cain rubbed his jaw where there was still evidence of faint bruising from his fight with Makai Inigo. The leader of the Omri had roughed him up good during the challenge for the claim of the Alulpo Soulstice Washington. Up until that moment, Cain hadn't been aware that the Alulpo weren't as rare as his people claimed.

If what Brody had claimed was true, Langsmith was swimming with Alulpo, and that made this assignment less a punishment and more a blessing in disguise. Too bad Cain was too much of an idiot to understand that.

"Langsmith it is," Cain grumbled and turned to leave the office.

"I didn't excuse you," Merwin snapped.

Cain stopped by the door and turned to face Merwin, his jaw twitched, and for a moment Merwin thought he would be foolish enough to attack him. Merwin may be a few centuries past his prime, but he was not going to be intimidated by such a young fool.

"You are to report to Brody, when you arrive. He will be in charge."

Cain shook his head.

"I'm not answering to that asshole."

Merwin stood, rising to his full height and letting his beast rise to the surface. His fingers elongated into sharp black claws that he traced down the edge of Cain's face.

"Your arrogance is a detriment, boy. Need I remind me just how quickly your fortunes can change?"

Cain glared at him, his own eyes turning into feline slits before he reigned himself in and nodded sharply.

"After this, consider my debt to you done. My fealty will be to me and me alone," Cain snarled.

Cain stormed out of Merwin's office. Slamming the door behind him. Merwin laughed at the young male's show of rebellion. It wouldn't last. Not once he realized that to get what he wanted in life, he would still have to play by Merwin's rules. Even Makai Inigo, the Omri bastard, knew not to push him too far.

***

Zazzie didn't open her eyes until she felt Hendrex collapse beneath her. They were no longer trudging through brush. Instead, they were in what appeared to be a one-room shack. Icarus leaned against one of the thin wood walls, breathing heavily and clutching his right arm.

"We'll be safe here for a while," he breathed.

Hendrex lay unconscious on the ground. Zazzie briefly panicked, but he was still breathing and didn't appear to have any major injuries. She reached out with her energy to his. He was weak and needed to rest in order to recover. She sagged against his body and cried.

Icarus sank to the ground, leaning his back against the wall to keep himself upright. Zazzie noticed thick streams of red blood dripping down his forearm.

"How bad are you hurt?"

Icarus looked up at her, his face pale and eyes glassy before they rolled into the back of his head.

"Shit!" she cursed and forced herself to move to him. His hand fell from his arm revealing a deep gushing wound. It was then she noticed the trail of blood to the door. He had probably bled a nice trail for anyone after them to follow. They couldn't stay here. Not like this, but there was no way they could move in this condition.

Zazzie tugged a length of fabric from her skirt and wrapped it tightly around Icarus's arm to create a temporary tourniquet.

With both men unconscious, there was nothing for her to do except find help. She didn't have enough energy to boost their energies with her own. She took a moment to steal herself before checking her clothing. her cell phone was still in her pocket, the screen cracked beyond use. She only hoped that the speaker function wasn't destroyed as well.

She tapped the voice assistant button on the side of her phone and spoke.

"Call Enora."

The screen flashed a few times before she heard the faint ringing. She teared up again, this time with relief. There may be hope for them after all.

"Hello? Zazzie?"

"Enora! I need help! I am in a shed somewhere in the woods beyond Fowler Park. Hendrex and Icarus are badly injured."

"Are you hurt? Are you okay?"

"I'm fine, just tired. Please, I don't know how long my battery is going to last, and my screen is shot to hell. Is it safe for me to make a run for it?"

There was a long pause before Enora spoke again.

"No! Stay where you are! I'll send help. Do you have enough energy to flare?"

"Barely," Zazzie admitted.

"Shit! Well, I don't know how safe it is. Do you think you can make it to nightfall?"

"I don't know."

Zazzie crept to the door and pulled it slightly open. Sure enough, there was a dark red streak of blood that led right to them, but the shed was covered in thick brush. There were no sounds around them, not even those of whatever woodland creatures lived in the area. That meant there were most likely Vampires on the prowl. Their unnaturalness would disturb the balance of the forest and keep the animals at bay. Sadly, that also meant Icarus's blood would draw them in like flies to shit.

"Enora, we can't wait. We're sitting ducks."

"Okay, just sit tight."

Zazzie shoved the door closed again and leaned her body weight against it. The tears continued falling down her cheeks. She closed her eyes and prayed to the ancestors that they would make it out of there safely.

"You have done well, Zenith, rest."

Zazzie found herself in the same grey room as

before, only this time instead of an altar, three beams of light spoke to her in unison.

"I can't, Hendrex is hurt, Icarus is hurt. I need to stay awake to keep them alive."

The lights flickered. In disapproval.

"Do you still doubt us? Do you not accept your purpose and our will?"

Zazzie fell to her knees, tears streaming down her face.

"I don't doubt you."

"A lie."

"I accept my purpose."

"A lie."

"I accept your will."

"A lie." The three lights flickered again, and Zazzie felt her energy draining from her body.

"What we give we can also take away."

"I'm sorry, but how do you expect me to trust in all of this?"

"You prayed to us, you asked for our guidance, and our aid. How dare you reject us now!"

"I don't reject you, I'm just confused."

"Then confused you shall be until you find the right path."

Everything went dark.

***

Sarah was helping to pass out medical supplies when Enora tapped her shoulder.

"Sarah, I need your help," Enora said.

Sarah set the medical supplies on the table and followed the pregnant doctor out of the trauma area set up to handle casualties from the battle.

"What do you need?"

Sarah did not know why she felt so connected to

the woman, but she knew in her heart that she would do anything to protect her and the child she carried as if they were related by blood.

"Zazzie is stranded in the woods. I need you to head a team to rescue her and two others."

"Have you cleared this with Tyr?"

Normally, Sarah wouldn't care. She relished the opportunity to be out in the field, but Tyr had effectively benched her since the fall of Ceres.

"No, there isn't time. They are injured and surrounded by Vampires. I hate to ask this. It's dangerous, but you are the only person I trust to help."

Sarah nodded in understanding. Tyr would not be happy about it, but what Enora said was true. They had taken heavy damages, and key personnel still weren't accounted for.

"Where are they?"

Enora relayed the information to Sarah, and she grabbed her bag.

"I'll call when I have them safely to the compound. That's closer than bringing them into the city.

"Thank you, Sarah."

Sarah pulled out her phone and dialed Kennan's number.

"You've been activated."

"You're shitting me," Keenan said.

"Nope, meet me at the rec center. We have a rescue mission."

Minutes later, Sarah met up with Keenan, Daphne, and Piran outside the rec center. They met next to the Community Unity Mural, the faces of some of the fallen from the Vampire attack were incorporated into the rainbow of graffiti. The wall was lit by a lone lamp, despite the sun still being out. Piran leaned against the wall chatting with Keenan while Daphne paced in front of them like she could already sense the danger they were about to step into.

The energy surrounding them was nervous and erratic enough to have Sarah tamping down her own shifter energy. It was weird for her to feel so out of tune with her animal and with herself. She hadn't felt this out of control since she had first turned. Yet, now could be seen as a similar situation. She was dealing with a new power that was both unknown and dangerous, and going on missions that could be life or death to those she cared about.

Sarah eyed her friends once more before approaching. Would she have preferred a more seasoned bunch? Hell yeah, but there were few others she would trust with this sensitive unsanctioned mission.

They were a rag-tag bunch, but they each had their own unique skills that would work well for what they needed to do and they were the only ones Sarah trusted not to rat her out to Tyr. Keenan and Daphne were Aura, so they had skin in this game, but Piran was a fellow Shifter and if he hadn't already made it clear that if she ever left the Langsmith pack he would follow as her Beta, then he wouldn't have been included. He had no idea about Sarah's energy abilities, and she planned to keep it that way as long as possible.

"We'll need to take Keenan's car to the edge of the wood. We won't be able to retrace their steps from the park for obvious reasons," Sarah began.

"I'll scan the area for energies. They will be weak, but I've been practicing," Daphne said.

"Great, that leaves me and Sarah to tracking and protection," Piran said.

"So, you are just going to leave me at the car?" Keenan whined.

"No, we'll need you to help with getting them to

your car. I am not strong enough to carry three possibly unconscious adults."

Keenan nodded.

"This isn't going to be easy. The woods are going to be swarming with Rogue Vampires. Hungry Rogue Vampires."

"Perfect," Daphne smiled.

Sarah shook her head, and they loaded into Keenan's car. It was time to get going. They didn't have much time; Sarah was sure of it.

***

The first thing Zazzie noticed when she woke was that she was no longer laying on a dirt covered floor. She panicked, her vision was a little blurry, but as it cleared, she realized where she was.

"Good, you're awake! I was worried I would have to find another teacher," Sarah said, appearing by her side.

"Where are Hendrex and Icarus? Did they make it?"

"Hendrex is resting in the other room, and Icarus was taken to the infirmary for his arm to be treated."

Zazzie sat up slowly. "Take me to him."

Sarah shook her head. "You need to rest. Aren't you the one who taught us not to deplete your core energy?"

Zazzie snorted.

"Do as I say, not as I do."

Sarah placed a hand on her shoulder and held her firmly in place on the bed.

"No can do. Besides, Daphne and Keenan have been taking turns helping him recover. There is nothing for you to do but rest and make sure you are okay."

"Why are you so adult for your age?" Zazzie grumbled.

Sarah's smile faltered for a moment before she turned away.

133

"I'll leave you to rest now. Just take another hour or two, and I'll be back to help you see him."

Zazzie relaxed into the bed.

"Fine," she muttered. "And Sarah?" She waited for Sarah to turn around.

"Thank you!"

"It's really no problem," the teenager said and then left Zazzie alone.

As much as Zazzie knew she should rest, she couldn't. Every time she closed her eyes, flashes of the carnage invaded her thoughts. Even when she tried to connect with her energy, there was almost nothing there, almost as if it had never existed at all. Sarah was right. She had pulled too much from her core energy. It would be a long time before it recovered, if it recovered at all. Tears flowed down her cheeks. She never wanted to feel this helpless again.

The door to the room opened again, and Enora entered. Upon seeing her friend, Zazzie tried and failed to get a handle on her emotions. Enora crossed the room and pulled her into a tight hug.

"Shh, it's okay. I'm here for you."

"Correction, we are here for you," Farrah said.

Farrah stood in the doorway with Disrayan. Disrayan leaned on Farrah's shoulder. She didn't have any visible injuries, but her energy levels appeared practically nonexistent. It seemed Zazzie wasn't the only one who overdid it. Zazzie was just glad they had all made it out of there alive and generally well.

Disrayan and Farrah joined Enora and Zazzie on the bed. Group hugs were something they had rarely done as adults, but had recently started to become a thing as each of them had struggled with their new reality. This time it was for Zazzie's sake. They sat in silence, bathing in the comfort of each other. Not a dry eye in the room.

"This is just the beginning," Farrah whispered.

"Which is why we all need to be more careful," Disrayan said.

"This isn't the world I wanted to bring new life into," Enora said.

Zazzie sighed.

"Maybe we should try to recreate Ceres. I know how much we all felt stifled before, but now I can't help but think maybe we were wrong. That maybe this was exactly what our Elders were trying to protect us from."

Farrah pulled away, shaking her head.

"No! I mean, yes, this was what they were trying to protect us from, but there are so many things we have gained from leaving the Sanctuary. If we somehow find a way to cloister ourselves, what was all this for? We've all sacrificed so much. So many have died fighting to live."

"I think that's the point, Farrah. While I agree it isn't the best idea to recreate the very system that created our circumstances, we shouldn't be opposed to closing the ranks either. It's clear that we will never be able to live in peace with the Vampires," Disrayan said.

"Yeah, fuck Vampires," Enora muttered.

"Fuck, basic bitch Vampires. I can't say all Vampires are bad, and neither should either of you. We've all benefited from the alliance with Maura's Men," Farrah clarified.

"True, Xander, Claude, and even Shane have come to our aid many times. You shouldn't call them Maura's Men, though," Disrayan said.

"Fine, the dark ones," Farrah laughed.

"All Vampires have dark energy," Enora said.

"Not as dark as theirs, but I agree the dark ones doesn't sound right either," Zazzie said.

"It doesn't matter. What matters is we are all safe,

and we need to keep it that way. Even if it means leaving Langsmith," Farrah said.

The room fell silent again. Leaving Ceres was one thing, but Langsmith had a pull that none of them could deny. There was a reason so many Supernatural gathered in the area. There was literal power in the air. A commotion outside broke the silence.

"What the hell is going on?" Tyr's voice boomed through the space.

"Sir, there are Aura at the gate. They are demanding we return their people," a male voice said.

"Demanding?" Tyr's Alpha energy crackled through the air.

"I better go check things out," Farrah said.

"I'll come with. I am Ruling Council, after all," Disrayan muttered.

"I better go too. I need to check on the other injured," Enora sighed.

They gave Zazzie one last squeeze before slipping out of the room. Zazzie knew she should probably stay put, but her curiosity got the better of her. Slipping out of the bed, she gingerly made her way to the door. Her energy was so depleted, the short walk was enough to have her leaning against the door frame to catch her breath.

The hallway was empty. Everyone having either moved into one of the rooms that lined the long hallway or gone outside to see what was going on. Zazzie made her way down the hall, stopping when she reached a large room. The front door was open and there was a small crowd gathered outside the door. No one paid any attention to her as she made her way to join them.

"We are not holding anyone against their will," Tyr said to someone Zazzie couldn't see. His massive frame blocked her view, but as soon as the other person spoke,

Zazzie knew exactly who it was.

"Regardless, there are Aura present that need to be in the care of our own. I appreciate your generosity in this manner, but it's time to hand them over," Jasmine Hyperion said.

"They aren't all stable enough to move," Enora interjected.

"Then, allow those who are to leave and prepare those who aren't for proper transport," Jasmine spat.

Disrayan and Jaq stepped forward.

"Ruling One and I have made the decision that they should stay until prepared to leave. We understand your hesitance to trust an outsider, but Tyr and his pack have proved to be trusted allies," Jaq said.

Jasmine looked Jaq over with disgust.

"More than two votes are needed to make such decisions," she snapped.

Disrayan stepped forward then.

"The Magistrate is unconscious, and Ruling Three expressed his wish to be treated as necessary before falling unconscious himself. I'm sorry you feel so pressed to react in this situation, but it has been handled. Please, do not disturb our allies further. Return home. What our people need is reassurance that things are under control, not this show of ego."

Zazzie loved watching Disrayan tear into people, but she garnered an additional joy that it was Jasmine Hyperion on the receiving end. To be truthful, there was nothing specific about the woman that Zazzie shouldn't like. She was a great instructor; she took her job on the Ruling Council seriously. Maybe it was because of the roadblocks Jasmine had insisted on throwing in Zazzie's pursuit to start a school.

Maybe it was lingering distrust from their younger years, when Jasmine took it upon herself to police everything she and the others did. It was a wonder the woman never showed an interest in the Security Force with the way she loved to interfere with other people's business. Zazzie refused to believe her dislike for the woman had anything to do with her obvious preference for Hendrex. Could she blame the woman for wanting the unobtainable when Zazzie herself had done so for years? Whatever it was, Jasmine Hyperion would never be someone Zazzie could call a friend.

The discussion continued, but Zazzie had seen enough. She moved back inside and went on a search for Hendrex. Since she was already out of bed, there was no reason for her to return to it without checking on him first. She found his room two doors down from her own. He rested peacefully in bed. No trace of the usual furrow in his brow that marred his sleeping features. He was at peace for the first time in a long time, and Zazzie hated the irony of the fact it took injury and near death to ease him.

She crawled onto the bed with him, wrapping her limbs around his still body.

"Please, Hendrex. You can't leave me like this. I need you to wake up."

He didn't reply. Not that she expected him to. She lifted her head and pressed a kiss to his lips.

"Wake up, handsome," she whispered jokingly.

His lips twitched a little, a small smile forming before Zazzie felt his arm move up to hold her body in place on top of his. She hoped that meant he really was awake, but he didn't open his eyes or speak. Still, she took solace in knowing he recognized she was there. She snuggled into him, letting exhaustion claim her once more. Her eyes drifted closed.

***

A warm weight settled over his body, and the panic Hendrex had felt for the last few hours subsided. *Zarovia.*

He had regained consciousness a few hours ago but hadn't had the energy to open his eyes or even speak. At least now, he knew she was okay. Meeting at Fowler Park had been a mistake. He should have insisted that Icarus meet him elsewhere. It was a shame they had underestimated the Vampire threat.

Now wasn't the time to reflect on yet another failure of his to protect Zazzie. He needed to let himself rest and regain his strength. The battle had taken a toll, not just on him, but on the Aura as a whole. He had no idea how Icarus was doing, which could only mean the Ruling Council was probably in shambles once again.

Hendrex focused on the soft inhale and exhale of Zazzie's body. Mirroring her breathing patterns, he felt his body relax further. Even though his energy was nearly depleted, he could feel himself reaching for hers. The normally bright energy was fine and pulsating weakly within her. Not much stronger than his own.

Still, what little energy they had connected in a dazzling spectacle of color, feeding off each other, and yet, somehow growing stronger as they did so.

Mine.

The thought danced in his head. He knew they belonged together before, but the way their energy melded and grew together, there was no denying they were in fact made for each other.

After a few moments, Hendrex felt himself falling back to sleep. A smile crept across his lips.

Hendrex was back on the cliff edge overlooking the valley. Langsmith was a smoldering pile of ash. The earth rumbled beneath his feet and the ground began to give way. Hendrex reached to his left, finding Zazzie's arm. He pulled her into his embrace. A wrapped bundle in her arms cradled between them.

"It's okay. We shall live on," Zarovia said.

The bundle in her arms cooed softly, but her reassurance did nothing to ease the panic growing in him as the ground fell from beneath their feet.

They fell, holding each other.

Hendrex jerked awake. Zazzie was no longer pressed to his chest but snuggled at his side, sound asleep. He wiped the sweat from his brow before reaching for the glass of water left at his bedside. He had no idea what this reoccurring dream was about, but whatever it was, he didn't like it.

Even if it showed the promise of a family with Zazzie, they were by no means in a safe or happy place. The world had literally crumbled and fallen beneath their feet, just as it had in Ceres.

Were the Aura so doomed? Were they never meant to be safe in the human world or even one of their own creation? Then, there was the question about the space ship. Hendrex knew much of Aura history, and while otherworldly beings were briefly mentioned, they were not mentioned in friendly terms. Of course, it could all just be a metaphor for the unknown that they all faced.

Hendrex swung his legs over the side of the bed. He still felt weak, but much better than when he first awakened. As much as he would have loved to continue resting by Zazzie's side, he knew there was too much work to be done. He carefully tested his weight on his legs. He sighed with relief when they didn't immediately give out. After taking a few cautious steps, Hendrex was sure he could get around enough to find Tyr or someone who could give him an update on what had happened while he was unconscious.

***

Mack sat across from Tyr, Xander, and Donovan. They sat in silence, contemplating their next steps. Instead of meeting at the warehouse where they usually held meetings, they were holed up in one of the gathering rooms on the Shifter compound. There was no point in hiding their connection now that shit had literally hit the fan for all parties involved.

"I won't be able to keep this from the Shifter Council," Tyr said, sitting back in his chair.

Mack nodded.

"Sorry, man. I knew I should have stopped Hendrex from going."

"It's not your fault. The Rogues haven't been this brazen since the original attacks. There was no way of knowing it would turn out like this," Xander said.

"Speaking of the Rogues, any headway with the Vampire Council?" Donovan asked.

Xander shrugged. "They are understandably wary of placing trust in me and the others."

Jaq strolled into the room, followed by Hendrex. Mack stood and rushed over to give his brother a hug. It was uncharacteristic of him, but given the circumstances, necessary. He'd nearly lost his other half.

"You shouldn't be up so soon," Mack said.

Hendrex smirked and pushed him away.

"Don't go soft on me now, Maclovis. I'm fine."

Hendrex took a seat at the table with the others. Mack studied his brother. He was indeed better, but far from fine. His energy levels were good for an average energy wielder, but not for someone of Hendrex's caliber.

"What did I miss?" Hendrex asked.

"Jaq didn't fill you in?"

"We just ran into each other at the door," Hendrex said.

"The attack was a coordinated effort by multiple

Rogue Vampire clans. They didn't know Icarus, but as soon as Hendrex arrived, they put out the call."

"Shit," Hendrex cursed.

"Welcome to the club, cuz," Jaq laughed, but it wasn't from humor. There was a defeated edge to his voice.

"You've made the list, Hendrex, and now, so have many others. It's only going to get worse from here on out," Xander said.

Tyr sat forward.

"Who is your source in the Rogue Vamps?"

"The rumor mills. Despite the turmoil, Molly's club is still the rumor mill super highway. It's the one neutral place in town. Well, fairly neutral now."

Jaq nodded.

"Maybe we need to meet with the Rogue leaders and broker a truce. I know I'm usually the first to jump into a fight, but I've got a child on the way. I can't risk any harm coming to them," Jaq said.

Mack smiled.

"I'm glad to see Binding has matured you," he said.

Jaq flicked him off.

"It's not a bad idea. If we can set a meeting, maybe we can settle this once and for all," Xander said.

Tyr shook his head.

"Rogue Vamps can't be trusted. Their word is hardly trustworthy."

"You want this to keep happening? We're on the radar of the human authorities now. Our glamour may have shielded the main action, but the remnants of the battle are hard to explain, given what was seen by passersby," Donovan said.

"Not at all. All I'm saying is that meeting with the Rogues probably won't give you the outcome you want. If anything, they might see it as a sign of weakness and attack again," Tyr said.

"We can handle them," Jaq said.

"Not right now, we can't. We've had too many casualties and are too open to exposure right now. Everyone is on high alert," Mack said.

"How many have we lost?" Hendrex asked.

The table went silent.

"We have six dead, so far. Mostly humans from The Resistance, but we lost one Aura and one Shifter."

"So far?"

"Plenty were injured and have recovered, but there are those who haven't yet. Icarus being one."

"Shit!" Hendrex cursed.

"Yeah, it's not looking good. We have few options on how to act. This wasn't entirely an unprovoked attack, since you both ventured into what has firmly become their territory."

"We met at a park! How is that a declaration of war?"

Mack shook his head. He'd never seen his brother this visibly upset. Another sign he wasn't recovered enough to be in this meeting. His head wasn't clear enough for this.

"I think what's best is that we focus on the health of our people and focus on our defensive measures."

"I agree," Xander said.

Jaq and Tyr exchanged looks before both nodded their heads in agreement.

"We are all too raw for any real decisions right now. The Rogues will also be distracted with regrouping and driving up their numbers. Besides, the Rogues are only one issue facing us at the moment. We need to be sure we have something worth fighting for in the first place," Mack said.

Mack internally cringed at how much he sounded like his brother in that moment. Not that Mack wasn't concerned with the plight of the Aura, but he'd spent so many years outside of the fray that his speech sounded like something he took straight out of Hendrex's mouth.

"So, it's settled. We will all withdraw and take care of our own until we are in a position to move forward together. Tyr, please let us know if our assistance is needed with the Shifter Council," Xander said and stood.

There really was no use in them sitting around like a bunch of cuckolds. Yet, there was no real action they could take when so unprepared. With the meeting officially ended, Mack stood and yanked Hendrex from his chair.

"Alright, time to get you back to bed."

Hendrex pulled his arm out of Mack's hand.

"I'm fine. I'm going to go check on Zazzie."

Mack nodded with a smile. At least, his brother had some sense of priorities. Speaking of, Mack pulled out his phone and dialed Disrayan's number. She'd gone back to the Factory to deal with the mess Ruling Two had stirred up after the battle. He wasn't surprised when she didn't answer. Instead, she sent him a text saying she was busy and would call when she was on her way home.

Shaking his head, Mack dialed Greg's number. It would be hours before Disrayan was free, and he wanted to check in with Greg about Carrie's help. It seemed Greg wasn't as involved with Xander and the others as they had led them all to believe. If Xander couldn't get through to the Vampire Council, surely Carrie could, and if anyone was going to convince her to help them in their plight, it would be Greg. They may dance around it, but Mack was certain their connection was much more than what Greg liked to call battle buddies.

***

Zazzie woke as soon as her body registered that

144

Hendrex was no longer by her side. She stretched carefully, rolling out the kink in her neck from the awkward position she'd settled. She felt more rejuvenated after sleeping by his side than all the hours she'd spent alone in her own room. With a smile on her lips, she slid out of bed.

If Hendrex was up, then they could go back to her place. As soon as she had the thought, she pushed it aside.

I shouldn't be so eager to run from responsibility. I am the Zenith, after all, and this was a major blow to my people.

She went back to her room and found her things. Her phone was completely dead, but she could charge it later. Right now, she needed to find Sarah and get a better idea of what had happened. She didn't bother putting on her old clothes. They had been cleaned, but Zazzie was going to burn them as soon as she got back to her place. They were tainted for her now, too many traumatic memories that even a good sage cleanse couldn't rid them of.

She shoved them into her purse and set out to look for Sarah. Zazzie hadn't been to the compound before, and it soon became clear that the Shifters weren't exactly open to her presence there. She couldn't blame them either. It was her people's fault they'd been dragged into this mess. Shifters typically kept to themselves, preferring to gather information and stay neutral in conflict. Yet they actively took part in battle against Rogue Vampires and aided a people they were told were nothing but myth.

It didn't take long for Sarah to find her as she wandered around the compound.

"Hey! You shouldn't be up!" Sarah chastised, taking her arm.

Zazzie sighed.

"I'm fine. I just wanted to check in with you and see what happened. No one else will talk to me, let alone tell me what's going on."

Sarah bit her lip and looked around warily.

"Let's just say, not everyone is as open to helping as Tyr and myself. Come on, I'll take you back to your room, and we can talk while I arrange for your transportation back into town. I'd take you myself, but Tyr has been super strict about any Shifters going off compound right now."

"That's understandable."

Zazzie allowed Sarah to guide her back to her room.

"So first, the casualties were a lot less than we anticipated. Many recovered pretty quickly, and only a few remain too injured to be sure just yet," Sarah said.

"Okay, what about the human authorities? Did we do enough to cover things up?

Sarah sighed.

"You did your best, but there were bound to be mistakes in such a chaotic mess. I only wish I had been able to help you all more."

"Don't worry about that. You were there for what you could do. It's bad enough that you haven't been allowed the normal life of a teenager. Don't make it harder for yourself by second-guessing what you have done. Most teens wouldn't have known how to help, let alone so willing to face such dangers."

"You'd be surprised. There are a lot of others that would have liked to help, they just don't have the same skills and control that training with you has afforded both me and Daphne."

Zarovia smiled softly.

"I get it, and I'm still working on it. Right now, we just don't have the space to train more than a few of you."

Sarah nodded.

"I talked to Molly after the battle. I think it would be okay if she wants to help."

Zazzie raised an eyebrow at Sarah. This was a complete one-eighty in attitude for Sarah toward Molly. The girl didn't trust easily, and Molly's dangerous amount of energy ability put any shifter worth their salt on edge.

"What about Daphne?"

"She's been hanging out with me more outside of class. She's coming around to some of the Vampires in The Resistance, so I think it could be safe to include Molly now."

Zarovia nodded, still unsure if she was open to the idea of training with the woman, let alone allowing her around any of the students.

"I'll think about it."

There was no way she was going to agree without feeling out the situation first. Molly might not even want to be part of the program after this conflict with the Rogue Vampires.

Sarah placed a hand on Zazzie's shoulder.

"Please do more than just think about it. I know I had my own misgivings about her, but so do most people about me."

There was no denying Sarah's request now. With a sigh, Zazzie acquiesced.

"Alright, I'll arrange a meeting with her."

Sarah smiled and then her ears perked up.

"Time to go! Be safe, okay?"

Sarah stood and walked Zazzie outside to the waiting car. A huge smile broke out on Zazzie's face as she saw Jaq and Enora.

"I'll call you when I have a new schedule for classes," Zazzie called.

She opened the door to the blacked-out SUV, and her smile widened as she saw Hendrex in the backseat. He looked up at her, and their eyes met. She blushed from ear to ear as she slid in next to him. Hendrex grabbed her hand before leaning in close and pressing his soft, warm lips to her cheek.

"I can't wait to get you home," he whispered in her ear.

Arousal flooded her, and she crossed her legs.

Hendrex chuckled and turned to look out the window. His thumb gently caressed the back of her hand. It was fine that they sat in silence as Jaq and Enora filled in the gap of conversation with their bickering about names for their baby.

As much as Zarovia loved working with kids, she'd never considered having any of her own. At least, not really. As they entered this dark period in Aura history, Zazzie wasn't sure she ever would. It would take years before there was any hope for peace, and it wasn't like the Aura way of life had been all that stable to begin with. Even in Ceres there had been uncertainty about the strength of energy one's child would have and what that would mean, not only for their future but the future of a family.

Shaking her head, Zazzie focused on the present. They had never talked about their relationship with any sort of future. It had always been whatever felt right in the moment. There was no telling how things would end up. No, right now, she would focus on what she had control over and that was training her students to protect themselves in case of situations like what had occurred.

There should be no opposition from the children's' parents after what happened. Any parent should want their child prepared for such a scenario. She had been hesitant to push for more, but now, it wasn't just a hypothetical. If the families planned to stay in Langsmith, they would all need to be well-versed in controlling their energies. Especially the younger ones, who were most likely to be out and about in vulnerable areas.

"Penny for your thoughts?"

Hendrex brought her hand to his lips and kissed it. She turned to him and smiled.

"Just trying to figure out a space large enough and safe enough to accommodate all the new students I'll have after today."

Hendrex's smile faltered.

"I don't think that's a good idea."

It was Zazzie's turn to frown.

"Good thing it isn't your idea to second guess."

Hendrex glanced toward the front of the car. Zazzie looked up too and noticed Jaq and Enora had stopped their bickering to listen in.

"We'll discuss this later," Hendrex said, giving her hand what she was sure he assumed was a reassuring squeeze.

She pulled her hand away from his and turned back to looking out the window. They entered the city limits. For some reason, Zazzie had imagined it would look different to her. That there would be evidence of the turmoil roiling within, not the nearly pristine tree-lined streets and smiling human faces that greeted her as they passed through downtown. Maybe things weren't as bad as they thought.

***

Brody stood in front of the Vampire Council, a smug grin on his face.

"I will be filling Maximus's position," he announced.

The Vampires who had looked down on him for years all looked at each other before bursting into laughter.

"You can't be serious. Brody, now is no time for jokes. Who have the Royals really appointed?" Nathanial said.

Brody walked to Maximus's empty seat and sat.

"I was handpicked by Merwin himself."

Nathaniel's smile faltered and was replaced with anger. Fire danced in his eyes, but he quickly quelled it.

"So, what else have the Royals decreed?" Kirima spoke next.

Brody hadn't expected her to be so nonchalant about his new appointment, but it did make him feel a little better that she seemed to be behind him in all of this.

"The magic users of Langsmith are the property of the Royals. We are to facilitate in squashing their rebellion and return Langsmith to order. Their freedom here is only by the grace of their masters," Brody said.

"What Carrie said was true," Kirima gasped.

Nathaniel snorted.

"What? You thought Maximus was the only one with his hands in the pie? Kirima, get with the times. These Aura, as they call themselves, are the key to our success and fortunes. Their blood gives us power beyond what has been naturally given," Nathaniel said.

"I don't care what you do in your spare time, but I will not be party to such blatant atrocities." Kirima stood and left the room, leaving Brody alone with the rest of the Council.

"We need a plan," Brody said.

"Easy, find where they are hiding and round them all up. I can provide men and transport," Nathaniel said.

"It won't be that easy. I've been in Langsmith for a while now, and the magic users are amazing in their ability to hide," Brody said.

"The Rogues managed to bring them out in force, and we are much smarter than they are," Nathaniel said.

"They also brought out every other Supernatural being in Langsmith and exposed us all to the outside world. You're right, we are smarter than the Rogues, which means we should be able to come up with a better, safer plan for all of us."

"Then, what do you have in mind?"

Brody smiled, a tactic to buy himself some time. He hadn't quite figured that out himself. It was obvious these magic users had powerful allies amongst the Supernatural in Langsmith, and Merwin might not care what happened in Langsmith as long as he got his property, but Brody did. He could see the bigger picture.

"Jaquis Andromeda, he is their leader. Follow him, and we'll find the rest."

Repercussions

Mack sat across from Greg and studied the man. He was like a standard issue GI Joe figurine. The two of them together would look out of place anywhere, but even more so in the run-down bar that had quickly become their favorite meeting spot. It was off the beaten path and away from the areas most other Supernaturals frequented. It was the perfect place to have a drink and a friendly chat without worrying about all the ears and eyes. Which was especially important since the surge.

"Carrie is not taking things well. I'm worried about her," Greg said.

Mack nodded. He didn't honestly care how Carrie was doing. He still didn't trust her as an ally, especially now that they'd had at least a partial hand in killing her father. Still, he knew Greg was in deep with Carrie and acting as their intermediary with her had proved useful since that night.

"Worried about her professionally or personally?" Greg scowled and downed the rest of his whiskey before signaling the bartender for another.

"On the record, professionally. Off the record, both."

"So, where does that leave us? Is she still willing to approach the Council on our behalf?"

"I'm new to her world. Hell, I'm new to this whole Vampire thing in general. I wish I could give you a clear answer on this, but I can't. Carrie, while admittedly honest about her father's failings, is still grieving the loss of a parent. On top of that, as someone of her and her father's stature, there is this crazy old school grieving period in which she is basically expected to lock herself away for six months."

"So, that would be a no. The Vampire Council isn't going to wait six months to retaliate, and we both know it. Not only them, but the Rogue Vampires moving in to fill the power vacuum left in the area. We can only blame so much on Maura and her would-be army before the MO stops lining up in a plausible way for the human authorities."

Mack paused to take a sip of his own drink.

"We can't even rely on Enora's help for much longer. One of the detectives is already suspicious and, in her condition, we only have a few more months before she goes on leave."

Greg nodded.

"This whole situation sucks."

"That's putting it mildly."

They drank the rest of their drinks in a commiserating silence. Mack had the disheartening feeling that his efforts to maintain peace were for naught. There were too many grenades to juggle for there to be any chance of avoiding all the impending explosions.

The silence was broken by the soft trill of Greg's phone. He looked at the screen, and the slight blush that crept across his pale skin let Mack know exactly who was calling. He shook his head and dropped a few bills on the table to cover their drinks and the tip for the bartender.

"I guess it's time to go face the music," he muttered, but Greg wasn't listening.

He was already heading out the door whispering into his phone.

Mack nodded at the bartender before following Greg out. The bright sunlight was a shock to his system after the dimly lit bar. Shielding his eyes, he pulled out his own phone. He expected to see a message from Hendrex, but there was nothing. Despite being twins, they had never been super close; their lives had always seemed to be on such different paths. Still, Mack was prepared to make the effort to help his brother acclimate to life outside of Ceres. Their call earlier had been cut short, but Mack knew exactly where to find his brother at this time of day. Stuffing his phone back into his pocket, he started the walk to the Factory. The new Aura headquarters. His jeep was parked right in front of the bar but he would have to come back for it when he sobered up. Besides, the walk to the Factory would give him a good chance to survey the energy around town.

Things had been understandably uncomfortable the last few weeks. So much had happened in such a short time period, and everyone was on edge. Not just the Supernatural community, but the human population as well. A serial killer, and now a mass murder that was blamed on increasing gang violence. The once busy streets of Langsmith had grown silent as an eerie calm settled over the city. It wasn't the refreshing kind of calm either, but definitely the expectant calm of anxiety before a storm. Mack could only hope he was taking the right steps to help prepare, not only himself but his people, for that storm. It would come sooner than any of them expected.

***

Hendrex couldn't wait to get out of the car. Zazzie was shutting him out, and he wanted to know why.

They had had disagreements before, and she'd never closed down so quickly. Not even after the incident with Jasmine. She usually was ready for a spirited debate, but then, maybe she was still too tired.

Asshole, she was hurt too. Now wasn't the time for petty squabbles.

He reached for her hand but she moved it away again, refusing to look at him. Even when Jaq pulled up to Zazzie's home, Zazzie thanked Jaq and Enora and took off without a glance in his direction.

Hendrex climbed out after her, but Enora grabbed his arm.

"Word of advice. Don't try to get in her way when it comes to the school. It's been her dream for so long."

"Thank you, I will take that under advisement," Hendrex said, offering Enora a soft smile before following Zazzie into her home.

At least, she hadn't locked him out. That would be a sure sign he had overstepped, and he would hate to have to further put Mack out by staying with him at Disrayan's while he and Zazzie figured things out.

Unlike the brilliance outside, Zazzie's house felt stale and depressing. Zazzie had already disappeared into her room, and as much as Hendrex wanted to follow, he knew he needed to have a game plan before he approached her. It would do no good to go in there half-cocked and end up saying something she would take the wrong way. So instead, he set about tidying her front room space. He opened the drapes and windows, letting both light and fresh air into the space. He finished cleaning the mess left in the kitchen from the last time they were there. At least, he had finished cleaning the dishes.

He placed the dishes back where they were supposed to be and went around checking the wards Zazzie kept around her house. She had let him help with them twice now, so he knew what do. By the time he was done, he still hadn't come up with a plan, so he went with the easiest one. He would just be honest with her about his feelings and his misgivings. It wasn't that he wanted her to give up her dream of opening a school. He just wanted her to weigh the cost benefit. Especially now, during an active conflict.

Hendrex found Zazzie lounging in her bath, cocooned in the glow of candles, the scent of tea tree and jasmine heavy in the air. Hendrex stood in the doorway enjoying the view of her naked body submerged in the scented water. She looked peaceful and relaxed, but he knew she wasn't asleep as her hands lazily ran along her skin. He smiled wondering if she planned to pleasure herself in the bath and if he should announce his arrival. He decided against the latter.

Her slim fingers grazed her collarbone before dipping down to cup her breast, her thumb and index finger wrapping around its peak, pinching and twirling her nipple. She gasped, and her eyes fluttered open, landing directly on him.

"You just going to stand there?"

That was all the invitation he needed. Hendrex stripped out of his clothes and stepped into the tub with her. The clawfoot tub wasn't exactly big enough for the both of them, but once she shifted to let him slide in behind her, they squeezed right in.

"I'm sorry I upset you," Hendrex said, rubbing his hands along her thighs.

"I don't want to talk about that right now," she breathed, dipping her hand low and grabbing his cock.

"Fair enough," Hendrex hissed before trailing kisses along her shoulders.

She stroked him long and hard, her tiny fists sliding up and down his shaft, which was cradled between her thighs. Her slick inner lips teasingly touching but not sliding over him the way he wanted. He grabbed her thighs, pulling her deeper into the water and positioning her where she couldn't avoid her clit coming into contact with him as she stroked him. He so desperately wanted to be inside of her, but he would maintain control over himself. When he was inside of her again, it wouldn't be at half energy. When they came together, it would be as two whole and complete entities merging into one.

Just the idea of it was enough to send Hendrex over the edge. He groaned as his seed spilled over her hands and into the warm water.

"Done so soon?"

Hendrex wasn't at all going to take the bait to argue like she wanted. He may be spent, but that didn't mean he couldn't give her all the pleasure she could handle. He slid his hand up her thigh to cup her sex. He placed two fingers at her core before pressing his palm firmly against her clit.

"Not nearly," he said and plunged his fingers inside of her.

Zazzie's hips raised to meet him, and he couldn't help but chuckle as he felt the tell-tale twitch of her inner muscles. She wouldn't last long either, but he wanted to see her face when she came for him. With his other hand, he grabbed a rag and her body wash. He used one hand to play with her, keeping her on the edge of oblivion, as he cleansed her body with the other.

"Why don't you just fuck me already?" Zazzie moaned.

Hendrex pressed a kiss to her cheek.

"I don't want to fuck. I want to make love, Zarovia, and neither of us have the energy for what that entails."

"You're too controlling. Love isn't something you control, it's something you feel in the moment."

"And you're telling me you feel love right now?"

He paused the movement of his fingers. Part of him wanted her confession, but the other knew if she confessed now, it would have more to do with his fingers teasing her G-spot and less to do with her actual heart. Sure, they'd admitted they'd wanted each other for years, but the word love hadn't been used on purpose. They were both too realistic to make such an assumption, no matter how strong their draw to one another.

"That is an unfair question, and you know it."

Somehow, that answer hurt more than he thought it should. It was an unfair question of him to ask, yet the fact she hadn't at least assured him of her attraction to him was a direct blow.

"It is, but it's a necessary one. I don't want to overstep with you, Zarovia. I care about you too much to treat this as a hot and heavy fling. I want more than that, and I want you to want more than that."

"I do want more than that."

Now that's better.

"Yes, but I think we can both agree we aren't ready for that kind of commitment. If things hadn't happened the way they did, I don't think we would be living together like this, do you?"

"No, but that doesn't matter. These are our circumstances. Unless," she turned to him, "Do you not want to be with me? Do you want your own space?"

Hendrex pulled his hand from her body. It was his fault for bringing up this conversation.

"I don't feel wholly a man living off of you, Zazzie. I want to say I'm okay with this situation, but I can't. It's just not how I was raised."

That was the mood killer right there. He felt her withdrawing again, and when she stood and exited the tub without so much as a glance back at him, he knew he'd fucked up. He reached forward and pulled the plug on the tub.

Did I just pull the plug on us like I did this tub?

When he finally emerged from the bathroom, he found his belongings piled neatly by the bedroom door and Zazzie nowhere to be found, he knew he had.

"Shit!"

***

It had been mere days, but it felt like weeks. No, it felt like years. Carrie sat in front of the window overlooking the street. The storm overlaying Langsmith was finally clearing, at least the one involving the weather. The storm in the Supernatural world, however, was just beginning. The Vampire Council would be appointing a new head of the region soon. If Carrie knew who was on the shortlist for the position, it would make it easier for her to lobby on behalf of her friends.

Not that it would be easy. No Vampire, neither born or turned, could overlook the direct attack upon her father—no matter the atrocities nor the injustices that befell Langsmith under his rule. Carrie pulled the soft wool blanket over her shoulders and looked down into her now tepid cup of tea. She had never felt more alone.

Carrie picked up her phone. It had remained mostly silent since her trip to Oracle. A few text messages from Greg that she replied to with lukewarm answers. Platitudes, so he would give her this time and days to figure things out on her own. As much as she valued input, she needed to learn to be more independent, and relying on Greg was all too easy.

Asking Greg to be her bodyguard had been a split decision. On the one hand, she wanted him around. On the other, her reasons weren't really reasoning at all. As much as she would like to be independent, she still

159

couldn't fathom being truly alone. It was unfair of her to ask Greg to be a part of her life without giving him all the details, but it was too late to change that now. Well, almost too late.

"Stop being a wuss, Carrie. Just call him."

She unlocked her screen and pressed his contact icon before she could chicken out again. The phone rang once before he answered.

"Where are you? I'm on my way."

Carrie sighed and shook her head.

"I'm at home, no rush. I just wanted to check-in and see how you are doing."

The phone was silent for a second.

"I'm fine. I'm more worried about you. How did things go with your family?"

"I already told you."

Greg chuckled, but it wasn't in amusement.

"I'm at your front door. You can tell me the truth when you come downstairs."

The call dropped. Carrie couldn't help the flush of warmth that spread through her body at the thought of Greg downstairs. And that was precisely the problem. Just a few weeks before, she thought herself head over heels for Shane. Now, she was crushing on yet another unavailable man. She needed to get her act together.

Despite knowing all of this, Carrie quickly flounced down the stairs to greet Greg in the entryway. She rushed him, and he welcomed her with open arms. Pressing her against his chest, Greg pressed a gentle kiss to the top of her head.

"I missed you. I know I'm supposed to be professional about this. I know that this is not the time."

Carrie wrapped her arms around him and leaned into his embrace.

"You're right. Now is not the time. I'll make us both

some tea."

Greg reluctantly let her go and headed to the kitchen. His rejection stung, but she knew it was for the best. She also knew Greg wasn't a fan of tea, so she joined him in the kitchen and pulled down the small container of instant coffee she kept just for him.

"The Royal Vamps aren't going to be much help in this situation. As far as they are concerned, Langston can burn."

"I figured that would be the case. From my limited experience with Vampires, you guys are dead set on vengeance."

"I wouldn't necessarily call it vengeance," Carrie said.

"Doesn't matter what you call it. If some sort of truce can't be made, more people will die. I've been to war twice. This is just the beginning."

Carrie nodded. She knew he was right. Despite her age, she had been sheltered. His expertise and insight were valuable to her.

"What about the others? What are they planning?"

Greg turned away from her, focusing on the boiling teakettle. It had yet to whistle, but he pulled it from the stove anyway and poured the steaming water over the loose tea. He was avoiding her question. That wasn't a good sign.

"To be honest, everyone is still scrambling from the attack. It's chaos. On top of that, I'm not exactly in the loop."

Carrie cocked her head to the side.

"Did you have a falling out with the guys?"

"Not exactly. That was another thing we needed to discuss. It seems I entered our arrangement without all the details. That was an oversight on my part, which I intend to correct."

And there it was. Greg offered her the cup of tea, and Carrie carefully brought it to her lips. The hot liquid stinging them, not so much because of the temperature but because of how he looked at her. She could feel he was conflicted about this. She set her cup down and sighed.

"Our agreement is exactly as presented. I can't help what others read into it or assume."

"No, but you could have warned me."

"I'm sorry."

Her gaze dropped to the counter before she moved to grab the kettle of water. Her movement was too quick, and instead of grabbing the leather-wrapped handle, her hand gripped the hot metal instead. It scalded her hands. She shrieked and dropped the kettle of hot water, splashing it across the counter. Yet miraculously, not a drop of the water reached her skin. Greg had quickly swept her into his arms and out of harm's way. He hissed as the hot water burned his flesh.

Without thinking, Carrie raised her wrist to her mouth and bit into it. She shoved her now bleeding arm to his mouth. She was surprised when he resisted at first. He had always been cautious when taking her blood but had never rejected her before. She pressed her wrist firmly against his lips.

"Drink! You need to heal."

Greg shook his head. "I'll heal just fine on my own. You shouldn't be so cavalier with blood-sharing."

He sat her unceremoniously on the ground before grabbing a towel and beginning to clean the mess. Carrie sat there in shock. Blood dripped from her already healing wound to the floor. Her entire body began to shake. A rush of unfamiliar emotion struck her. She clenched her fists, her fingertips digging into her palms. The urge she felt wasn't entirely one of anger. He was right, of course. The red blistering on his forearm was already diminishing to light pink welts.

Carrie wasn't sure how much time had passed as she sat there, battling her uncertainty. All she knew was Greg healed just fine, the mess she'd made was cleaned up, and Greg studied her with equal parts concern and worse, pity from where he leaned against the counter. His muscled arms crossed over his broad chest.

"I think you should go."

She didn't want him to leave. Carrie just wasn't sure what to do. He cupped her face in his hands.

"Look, this situation is new for both of us. Let's start over. I am your bodyguard. I am your friend. Call me anytime you need me. The only thing I ask is that you don't put yourself in such a compromising position on my behalf. I may be a new Vampire, but I am still a man. I can take care of myself. I know when to ask for help and when I can handle things on my own."

The floor became her new favorite scenery. She didn't dare bring her eyes up to look at him. The last time she had felt like this, she'd been a young girl scolded by her father. Not that Greg reminded her of her father. Greg was the furthest thing from her father. Even the fact that she was thinking about her father at this moment told her that she was not in the right headspace.

Changing the subject, the only viable option. She took a step back and, out of his grasp, forced her eyes up to meet his. Crossing her arms over her chest, she sighed deeply.

"I don't know much about the attack, except that it was bad for both sides. How much do you know, and how much are you willing to share with me?"

Greg straightened and cleared his throat.

"I will tell you everything I know. Then, we can work on a plan to help fix this."

Carrie gestured toward the living room. "I have a feeling this might take a while. You might as well get comfortable."

They went into the living room and sat across from each other on the couch. Carrie sat on one end, Greg sat on the other, but she turned so her knees would brush against his. Despite everything, she couldn't bear to be without his touch.

"The fighting at the park was bad. There were people who were lost on both sides. Not really both, but all sides. I wish I could say the Shifters are for sure on the same side as the Aura, that Maura's Men are for sure on the same side as the Aura. My training dictates that I shouldn't believe either group will put the lives of their people in danger unnecessarily. Right now, though, everyone seems to be working together."

"Working together on what?"

"As far as I can tell, Maura's Men are rallying to take over Langsmith for the Vampires. The Aura, despite some infighting, are on track to establish their place in the city. There is talk of starting a school, a safe space for their children to learn. As far as the Shifters, the local pack has basically adopted the Aura as their own, but that may change if the situation worsens. The Shifter Council has already been informed of what's happened, and they aren't exactly fond of Tyr's stance on it."

Carrie contemplated this new information. It seemed things were still bad but not as bad as she anticipated. As long as the Aura, the Shifters, and Maura's Men banded together, they had a chance against whatever the Vampires threw at them. At the same time, it made her choice desperately clear. She didn't have a choice. She would have to step up and take her father's place.

***

When Zazzie had packed up Hendrex's stuff and put it by the door, she'd been pissed but as she stood in front of the last place she ever expected to be, she wished she had stuck around to actually talk about what had just transpired between them.

It wasn't that she didn't understand. Wasn't she always the one who preached being good by yourself before trying to be good with someone else? If Hendrex didn't feel like a whole person, how could she blame him for being cautious with her? Sure, the circumstances weren't ideal for their courtship. Under other circumstances, Zazzie would definitely not have him staying with her without any level of commitment, and yet, here she was unable to commit and him unready to commit.

That was not why she was here, though. She'd called Molly as soon as she left her home to see if they could meet up. The last thing she expected was for the emphatic yes and immediate invitation to the Maura's Men Compound. Staring at the castle-like mansion on a massive overlook of Langsmith was enough to have her second-guessing the Aura strategy of hunkering down within the city limits. Apparently, the way to go about it was to have a massive swatch of land in the wilderness away from the daily hustle and bustle.

Too bad the Aura did not have the funding to make such a grand purchase. She cautiously lifted her hand to knock, but there was no need. Molly flung the door open, a huge smile on her face. Before she knew it, Zazzie was wrapped in a huge hug by the petite Vampire.

"I'm so glad you're okay and that you changed your mind! I have so many ideas, and I've been wanting to train with someone other than Mack," she gushed.

This bubbly version of Molly was a complete flip from the bringer of death and destruction aura she had exuded in their previous meetings. It probably didn't help that her riotous red curls were tied back and her make up free face was all peaches and cream with cherry freckles.

"I just wanted to hear you out. I haven't made my decision yet," Zazzie said.

Molly pulled back and cleared her throat.

"Of course, sorry, I got a bit carried away. This is business. I just don't usually do business at home."

Zarovia hated that she felt like such a heel for killing the woman's joy. She had no idea what Molly's story was, but it was obvious, it was a tragic one for her to be who she was.

"Why don't we start by getting to know each other first?" Zazzie said.

Molly's demeanor brightened immediately, and she took Zazzie's hand before dragging her down the long hallway to the biggest non-commercial kitchen Zazzie had ever seen.

"Do you like tea or ice cream? We don't have much else here, besides alcohol and blood, being Vampires and all," Molly said as if it were the most normal thing in the world to say.

"Tea is fine," Zazzie said.

Molly fixed them both tea and sat at the island across from her.

"So, I'm sure you would like to know my story. Like, how I came about my powers or how I became the only female turned of the infamous Maura."

Zazzie bit her lip.

"I'd be lying to say I wasn't curious. Mack is very tight-lipped about you guys."

Molly nodded.

"Mack is tight-lipped about everything. I mean, we've been friends for years, and now, there is this whole thing with Aura and a wife? The man sure knows how to compartmentalize. Is his brother the same way? I don't want to assume that you are dating or anything, but he's staying with you, so you must be close."

Zazzie took a nervous sip of her tea.

"Hendrex is even worse than Mack, to be truthful. As for our status, that is still to be decided."

Molly smiled softly.

"I totally get that. I love my Shane, but it's been a long journey for us."

"How did you end up being turned by Maura? I don't know much about her outside of rumor, but it was clear she preferred to turn males."

"Long story short, I was just a pawn in her long game. She never intended for her power to be transferred to me. I wasn't turned in a normal way. I was dead, like really dead, decapitated."

Tea almost spurted from Zazzie's nose as she choked on that revelation.

"She used dark energy to raise you from the dead. That's forbidden and dangerous for even the most skilled of Aura."

"Yeah, it was no party, for sure. The evil lingered, it changed me. I wasn't myself for a long time. Still am not fully myself, but I'm working on it."

"Okay, so these powers, how did they start? I need to know, so I can help you with controlling it."

Molly told Zarovia her whole story. Apparently, her strange abilities weren't just from her abnormal turn. Like most Aura teens, her energy abilities had begun to manifest around puberty, but being in a foster home, she had hidden them from everyone, including her best friend Cat. She'd even had dreams of being abandoned beyond a glowing purple door.

Zazzie had nearly lost it upon hearing that. That

alone was evidence that Molly was one of the lost ones. One of the children she had wanted to reach out to and help to avoid potentially dangerous situations for them. Molly was living proof of the dangers of a lost one growing up not knowing what they were.

Like most lost ones, if they didn't cultivate their talents, they eventually lost them, which is what happened to Molly until her rebirth. Zazzie refused to call it anything else, even with such tragic circumstances. Molly had been reborn and given a second chance to live the life she was destined for. Zarovia couldn't for the life of her not care for the woman after hearing her story. If there was any way Zarovia could help Molly find her true family, she would do it, but much of their records had been lost in the fall and Molly hadn't exactly expressed interest in meeting them.

"Molly, you didn't need to traumatize the woman to convince her to work with you," a female voice said from behind Zazzie.

It nearly startled her out of the stool. She whipped around and saw a Princess Tiana lookalike standing with a laptop tucked under her arm and a grim expression.

"Zarovia, this is my best friend and Xander's mate, Cat."

"Nice to meet you," Zazzie managed.

Cat laughed.

"It's nice to officially meet you, as well. Molly and Mack have both talked about your school idea. If you are ever looking for a technology teacher, feel free to give me a call. Also, Gretchen can cover human history if there is a need. I know Vampires aren't exactly welcome with the Aura, but we are friendly, I promise."

Zazzie was taken aback by the offer; what the woman said was right. The Aura weren't friendly with Vampires, and despite the help they had provided, it was clear that sentiment wasn't going anywhere anytime soon. Still, Zazzie wasn't going to turn down the offer outright.

"I will keep that in mind."

"Good, now that the formalities are over, I'll let you two get back to training. We should hang out sometime too. It gets a little boring all the way out here, and the boys are super picky with who they let through the gates."

Zazzie nodded.

"Me and my girls have weekly drinks. Maybe we can have a joint girl's night."

The invitation was out there before Zazzie really thought about it.

"That sounds nice," Cat said and left the room.

Zazzie turned back to Molly, who smiled brightly at her.

"You just got conned by Cat," she said and stood.

"What do you mean by that?"

"I mean, Cat wouldn't have come out here if she wasn't curious, and she obviously likes you, because if you thought I was scary before getting to know me, I have nothing on Cat. Anyway, we can do some light training in the courtyard. It's where we do most of our weapons training, so there is less risk of damaging anything expensive or irreplaceable. A hazard of dating a Vampire is all the damned antiques they hold on to," Molly laughed.

"I don't need to date a Vampire to relate to that. Before the fall, Ceres itself was the land of antiques."

"I'd love for you to tell me more about Ceres. I mean, I was possibly born there, and it would be nice to know where I came from."

"Sure," Zazzie said.

The courtyard was spacious, and true to Molly's word, free of anything liable to be expensive to replace.

"I know you've trained with Mack, but he's been

out of the loop with the Aura for a while and probably conditioned you for battle scenarios. I, on the other hand, focus on incorporating the energies into your daily life. Not just to protect yourself from outside threat, but also as a form of self-care."

"That sounds lovely. Frankly, I'm tired of blowing shit up and disintegrating things," Molly said.

"Yeah, we will definitely be avoiding that. You ready to start?"

"Hell yeah," Molly said.

"Good. Once I can be sure you can control your energies in a calm setting, I will feel more comfortable introducing you to the other classes with Aura students."

Zazzie settled in with Molly and began to guide her through a series of meditation and energy guidance exercises. Molly caught on fairly quickly, and Zarovia wasn't surprised to find she was very in tune with her inner energy, even if she had never tried to commune with it before. By the end of their session, Zazzie was comfortable enough with Molly's progress to suggest she join the next class with the students, whenever that might be.

"I'd love that as long as it doesn't cause any issues."

"Don't worry about that. If anyone pitches a fit, I'll handle it. You were Aura first. They can't condemn you for the oversights of our past."

"Thank you, Zazzie."

"No problem."

Soon after, Zazzie gathered her things and headed home. It was already dark, and the darkness in her house let her know Hendrex had left. The joy she'd felt at hanging with Molly quickly dissipated. So much for a happy home. Her once peaceful space felt emptier than when it was just an empty shell at purchase.

He needs this space. I need this space. We need this

space.

Zazzie chanted that mantra to herself as she settled into cold sheets, tears streaming down her face. She missed him already.

***

The room was silent, yet full of animosity. Disrayan sat to her left, and Jaq to her right. They glared at her. Jasmine wished she could say she was unaffected by the intensity of it all, and while she did a good job of maintaining a neutral countenance, her skin literally crawled like a million bugs squirmed under each of the eight layers.

"I will not back down on this. It is unacceptable that we are not caring for our own," she said.

Disrayan took a deep breath and steepled her hands together on the table. Jasmine braced herself for the verbal lashing she was sure would come. Disrayan had no issue with taking people to task when she disagreed with them as she disagreed with Jasmine now.

"It is unacceptable but necessary. We simply do not have the resources available to us, and the Greywulf pack has graciously offered their support. We need allies in this world. I know you are new to things out in the real world, but that is no excuse for your behavior toward those who would help us."

Jasmine released a breath. She had expected worse, but there were dark circles under Disrayan's eyes. It hadn't been that long since Disrayan had faced her own mortality. Having been kidnapped by Vampires and nearly lost to the blood slave trade. This situation was hardly one she could look over without it triggering some form of trauma for her. Yet another reason Jasmine felt she needed to step up. She may be new to the real world, but that also meant she wasn't resigned about its dangers. Not only because of the Vampire threat, but to the sanctity of the Aura way of life. If they relied too heavily on others, eventually, there would be cultural crossover and possibly even physical crossover.

If the Aura started to mate with other Supernatural, it could lead to the end of their line completely. Not to mention, the creation of abominations like that Molly woman. An Aura tainted by dark energies and even darker Vampire blood. Her power wasn't diluted because of her perversion, it made her more powerful. In the wrong hands, that kind of power and ability was dangerous. They would all be better off if Molly was the last of her kind. Jasmine couldn't say that, of course. That would only make it harder for her to get Disrayan and Jaq on her side. She needed to convince them slowly, but looking at the two of them, right then was not the time to try to make inroads.

"I did what was necessary. If any of you had bothered to inform me of your intentions, instead of running around like you don't have a responsibility to your own people, maybe this situation could have been avoided. The real question now is if you insist on starting fights with Vampires, how can we protect our people, let alone build the infrastructure needed when we are focused more on offense than defensive strategies?"

Jaq scoffed and rolled his eyes.

"You can read all the tactic manuals you want, Jasmine, but that doesn't train you for the real deal in the trenches kind of stuff. It's real rich, you over there talking out the side of your mouth about necessary infrastructure when I believe it was you who is behind the hindrance of Zarovia building a school for our kids. A school that would provide not only education but security for current and future generations. You can miss me with your high and mighty bullshit."

Jasmine straightened at the use of such foul and improper language at an official Council meeting.

"You only care about future generations now that you have a stake in that future. Yet here you are endangering it all over a so-called alliance with the Shifters. Do you think they will always be on our side? They have a history as observers, not participants. We can't rely on Tyr and his pack when at any turn they could withdraw their support."

"As much as I hate to admit it, Jasmine has a point. Tyr may be willing to help, but we've already seen that not everyone in his pack is on board with the idea of helping us out. Especially now that the Vampires are being so blatant and indiscriminate with their attacks," Disrayan said.

Jasmine smiled. Maybe Disrayan wasn't a lost cause as of yet.

"Precisely. Now, we need to get Icarus back. I understand he is in fragile condition, but we can't let one of our leadership be held this way. It makes us look too weak, too easy of a target. It does nothing to engender hope in our people that we will be okay."

Jaq stood from the table, shaking his head.

"Icarus is fine where he's at. If we try to move him now, we may as well announce a call for a new Ruling Three. I won't be a part of that. Now, if you'll excuse me. I have other shit to do today."

Jaq stormed out of the room, leaving Jasmine alone with Disrayan.

"I don't know why the people voted him into the Council when he shows nothing but disdain for the Aura and our traditions."

Disrayan smirked.

"Traditions that led us here in the first place. People are tired of living in fear. Jaq is the embodiment of living freely as an Aura in this new world and thriving. Is he deserving of that honorable place amongst our people, maybe, maybe not, but who are we to speak for the people in that regard? They put us where we are. They can take us from these pedestals at any point. Jasmine, I understand your point of view. I do. Tradition is important, but when is it okay to separate ourselves from traditions that do more harm than good?"

"Who are you to decide what traditions are harmful and which are not?"

"I could ask you the same," Disrayan countered before standing and leaving.

Jasmine sat alone in the conference room. Mulling over her thoughts. She could hear the storm raging outside, flashes of lightning lit the sky outside the window, heavy droplets of rain ran in sheets of water down the glass panes. Jasmine was filled with an overwhelming sense of dread. As if the ancestors themselves had brought along this storm in warning.

Mess

Icarus stood in the middle of a field. He'd walked for what seemed like ages and gotten nowhere. Nothing but blue skies and tall golden grasses as far as the eye could see. He spread his arms out wide and screamed in frustration.

Where the hell am I?

He closed his hands into a fist, and that's when he felt it. Nothing tangible at first, but the tighter he closed his fist, the more tangible it became. The warm sensation grew stronger, curling around fingers and his palm. The faint outline of a hand glimmered into existence. The first sign that he was possibly not alone. The hand tried to pull away, and as it did, it began to disappear again. He couldn't let that happen. He held on tight, as tight as he could, no matter how much the hand struggled to get away. Finally, it settled. Reveling in this new connection, Icarus brought the hand to his chest. As he did so, an arm formed, attached to the hand.

The skin was smooth and young looking, but he couldn't tell if it was someone he knew. Perhaps it was all his imagination. Either way, he was trapped in this place, with nothing familiar. He couldn't even connect with his energy here. Yet holding this hand, whoever it was, made him feel safe and connected to the real world once more. He would do anything to hold on, this had to be the way out of here. He concentrated on the hand, on the feeling of connection. The more he focused, the more tangible the person became, still more of a ghost figure, but definitely real.

Icarus was so intent on the figure, he hadn't realized the space around him was closing in. The blue skies turning grey and then black, the golden fields disintegrating around him. He wasn't paying attention to any of it. Only to her. The girl who saved him. He couldn't see her face, but she seemed somewhat familiar. Maybe she was an Aura teen sent to care for him. If so, he would owe her a great debt if he ever woke from this nightmare. On the other hand, she could be an angel, a guardian sent to guide him into the afterlife. To retrieve him from this blasted limbo and install him in his rightful place amongst the ancestors.

Icarus didn't think that was the case. He was still so young. He had only just started making his mark on the world. He never thought his mark would be that of a martyr. The darkness encroached even closer. He could feel its pull on his body, not pulling him away from the girl but toward her. He pulled her close and shut his eyes tight.

"I accept my fate. Whatever shall come will be," he whispered to himself.

***

Sarah put away the roll of gauze she had used to wrap up a wound from a training accident. She wanted to be out in the field where the real action was. Not stuck on the compound playing babysitter and trainer to the youngsters. Any other time, sure, but not right then. Not when there were still those on the loose who had hurt her friends and family.

"There's a storm headed this way. You interested in a rain run?"

Sarah smiled and turned to Sequoia.

"You know I hate the rain."

Sequoia laughed.

"Not as much as you hate being sidelined."

Sarah shook her head.

"You're right, but I'm not in a good place for a run today. I have to go explain to Ginger why her baby boy won't be shifting for the next week."

Sequoia winced.

"That bad?"

"Broke his arm in three places. He's still too new to shifting for it to heal during the change."

"Ouch, poor boy. Maybe I should be the one to tell Ginger. Cain is out of town, and she's still adjusting to pack life."

"Can you? I mean, I know it's my responsibility, but I don't think I can handle a weepy human on top of everything."

Sequoia pulled Sarah into a tight hug. Sarah hated them but Coy insisted on it and after hanging out with more humans and other Supernaturals lately Sarah was getting used to gestures of affection and care.

"Okay, I'll stop being all gushy. Why don't you invite a few of your friends over? You can watch movies in the living room, and I promise not to bug you."

"That sounds nice," Sarah said.

Coy smiled and headed out the door. Sarah was about to follow when she picked up on whispers from some of the Shifter women caring for Icarus.

"His wounds are healed? He should have woken by now?"

"Are they sure there was no other damage?"

"Maybe it's an energy thing. We are new to working with the Aura. Some of the others that took a while to recover complained of lack of energy."

"Yes, but he's had visitors. I saw them chanting over him like they did the others. I still feel like something else is wrong."

"Let's give him a day or two more to rest. We have others with wounds we can actually tend to."

The two women's footsteps receded down the hall. Curious, Sarah headed to Icarus's room. She had met the man exactly twice, once the night Ceres fell, and the second time as she carried his bleeding body to safety.

The room was dark, the sun having already begun to set, the small window in his room open to let the night air in. Icarus lay perfectly still, tucked tightly in white sheets. His face appeared calm and serene. Sarah checked the hall one last time before closing the door behind her. She was curious to see if his issue really was a lack of energy.

She pulled a chair up next to his bed and took his hand in hers. It was cool to the touch, as if there were little circulation reaching his thick fingers. She laced her fingers between his, rubbing and blowing on them to generate heat the way she had seen in human movies. She nearly fell out of her seat when his fingers curled around hers, grasping her tight.

She tried to pull her hand away, but he held it with a firm grip. Her eyes darted to his face; his eyes were still closed. His breathing still shallow. She focused, and she could feel and hear his heart beating stronger, with a more regular rhythm. She relaxed, allowing him to hold her hand. Maybe that was the problem. Maybe he just needed someone to be there. Sarah could relate to that. In her younger years, before she met Tyr, she had spent many nights alone, wondering if anyone would ever care about her. It was a feeling she still sometimes had, even with Tyr and Sequoia acting as doting parents.

"It's okay. I'm here. I won't go anywhere," she whispered.

She felt his grip relax, but he still held her firmly. She sat with him for about thirty minutes before trying to free herself. He still refused to let go. With a sigh, Sarah pulled out her phone and texted her friends. A movie probably wasn't happening tonight, but maybe if more people were around him, Icarus would finally wake, or at least let her hand go.

Sarah: Hey guys! I've got another mission for us.

Daphne: I'm stuck at home. The rents refuse to let me or my brother out of their sight after the attack.

Keenan: I can swing through if Tyr is okay with you hanging out alone with a man.

Piran: Alone? I'll literally be right there.

Sarah: Daphne, just sneak out; we know that's your thing. Kennan, if you even thought to try something, I'd handle you myself.

Daphne: I hate you.

Keenan: As long as I got to see you smile.

Piran: Again, what, am I invisible? Where we meeting?

Sarah shook her head. Sometimes, she wondered how she was friends with this rag-tag bunch.

Sarah: On the compound. I'm in the infirmary with Icarus.

Daphne: Icarus? Really? My parents might make an exception if I say I'm going to offer my respects.

Keenan: My heart. I thought I was your man. You got a thing for older men, don't you?

Piran: Be there in two.

Sarah put her phone away and rested her head on the side of the bed. She hoped it didn't take them long to get there. Her hand was getting cramped from being in the same position for so long. She had never held hands with a boy before, and granted, this was a different situation, but now, she wasn't sure it was something she would like. She only recently learned to open up to outsiders, to trust people again. This thing with the fingers laced was far too intimate, from the feel of the shared warmth to the slow pulse of their veins. It was too much. Sarah tried once more to pull her hand away. This time, she got her hand about halfway free before Icarus tightened his grip again and pulled her hand until it rested over his heart.

With a groan, Sarah adjusted her body to a more comfortable position. She slid off the chair and sat on the edge of the bed. Piran found her in the same position, and she could tell by the way his eyes darkened he was not amused by the situation at all.

"What the hell, Sarah?"

"Lower your voice, he's resting."

"Why are you in bed with him?"

"I'm not in bed with him. He grabbed my hand and won't let go."

Piran raised an eyebrow at her. He obviously didn't believe her. He crossed the room and tried to pull her hand from Icarus, but when he did, a bolt of energy shot from Icarus's other hand and zapped him.

"Ouch!"

"Holy shit!"

Sarah looked up to see Keenan and Daphne standing, mouths wide open, in the doorway.

"Uh, hi guys!"

Sarah tried and failed to hide the blush rising in her cheeks.

"So, what exactly just happened? I thought he was unconscious?" Piran rubbed his hand where he got zapped.

"He is," Sarah insisted.

"No way he's unconscious. He did that on purpose. You and him secretly having a thing?"

"Gross, no!"

Daphne crossed the room and placed a hand on Sarah's shoulder.

"It's okay if you do. I mean, yeah, he's older but not that much. You're almost eighteen."

"What kind of toxic romantic bullshit are you on? No wonder, your ass got kidnapped. He's a grown ass man. If he's hot for a seventeen-year-old, he's a pedo who needs to be outed," Keenan said.

"It's not like that. I don't even know him. I just came to check on him and this happened."

"A Shifter male knows his true mate upon sight. Is it the same for the Aura? Maybe he is instinctively protecting what he knows is his. I can respect that," Piran said, backing away.

Sarah rolled her eyes.

"None of you are listening to me. This has nothing to do with mating or romance. He was injured, and his friends are all too busy recovering on their own or trying to make things better out there, so he was lonely."

Keenan shook his head.

"Well, he ain't alone now, so why is he still gripping your hand like a love he never wants to lose?"

"That's why I called you all here. He is our mission. We need to show him he isn't alone, so he will wake up."

Piran laughed.

"That's some wishful thinking you have there. You go right on ahead, but I'm not messing with no mated, fucking Aura. I've seen and now felt what can happen when you cross one." Piran gave Icarus and Sarah a wide berth as he left the room.

Once he was gone, Daphne moved to the other side

of the bed and took Icarus's other hand. His fingers curled around hers, and it gave Sarah some relief. Her hunch was right, and her friends were jumping to conclusions because they were hormonal teens.

"Keenan, come on. Piran is gone. Let's try an energy circle."

Keenan looked like he was going to refuse, but he took Daphne's hand and then Sarah's.

"If bro wakes up and makes any kind of move on either of you, I'll rock him. I don't give two shits about him being Ruling Three."

"Noted," Sarah said.

"Okay, close your eyes and repeat after me. Once you have the words down, try to say them in tandem and focus on his energy."

"How do you know so much about healing chants?" Keenan asked.

"It's part of my individual studies with Ms. Monoceros. Now, focus."

Daphne began the chant. Almost immediately, Sarah felt the trickle of energy building in her palms. She mouthed the words until they felt right on her tongue before joining in with Daphne. Keenan took a little longer to get a hang of it, but soon, they found their rhythm. The energy built between them, but the trail seemed to stop at Icarus before bouncing back through them.

"It's not working," Sarah said.

"Shh, just focus. We aren't experienced with this, it's going to take a while," Daphne said before continuing with the chant.

Sarah sighed deeply before closing her eyes once more. She focused on reaching Icarus, more than channeling her own energy. At first, the results were the same but then she felt, slowly but surely, the energy being transferred into him as if each completed chant chipped away a brick in the massive wall blocking Icarus from the conscious world. His fingers warmed in her hand, his grip tightening as if he were using it to literally pull himself back to the present. Then, as quickly as it all began, it ended in an explosion of bright light. Sarah, Kennan, and Daphne fell back on their butts as Icarus surged up from the bed with a massive inhalation of breath.

***

He was alive! Weak and in pain, but alive! He was no longer in that dreadfully peaceful space, but in a room surrounded by three teenagers. Two he recognized immediately, and the third—he smiled and pulled the frazzled teen into a hug.

"You saved me!"

He was so overjoyed, tears streamed down his face. The girl struggled in his arms, and he let her go. Clearing his throat, he quickly wiped away the tears on his cheeks.

"I'll go get someone to check you out," the girl said and rushed from the room.

He was sad to see her go, but he understood. She'd just been there to watch over him while he was ill. It was her duty, and he had just hugged her as if his life depended on her being there. It had, but that was a lot to deal with for a teen. As it was, the two others stood by the foot of the bed he was in, the young girl staring in shock and awe, the young man glaring at him.

"Ruling Three, it's so great that you've recovered," Daphne said.

He knew it was her because the new Ruling Council had met with the family to offer apologies for the previous Council members' oversight regarding Daphne's disappearance. The boy next to her was Keenan. He was part of The Resistance, and Icarus had run into him a few

183

times when working with Jaq and Donovan to restructure the Security Force.

Icarus laid back down, exhaustion overcoming him now that the shock of waking had worn off.

"Thank you, I'm glad to have recovered. How long was I out?"

Keenan answered, "Three days."

"Three days? Has there been another attack? How many were lost?"

Daphne opened her mouth to speak, but Keenan shook his head at her.

"You should rest a bit more. The adults will be here soon to fill you in."

That was the truth. Icarus was tired, but also anxious. He settled in and took a deep breath. A moment later, the door swung open, and Tyr and Jaq were by his side.

"Hey man! Glad to see you're awake," Tyr said cautiously.

"Yeah, you took your dear sweet time getting back to us, man," Jaq said.

There was a bit of snark to the man's tone, but the look of concern overshadowed it.

"What did I miss?" Icarus asked.

"We can talk about that when your ass isn't laid up," Jaq said.

Icarus looked to Tyr, but Tyr only shook his head.

"At least, wait until tomorrow before jumping back into work."

"I feel fine," Icarus protested.

Jaq shot the two teens in the room a look, and Kennan took Daphne by the arm and dragged her out, closing the door behind them. Icarus was glad the teens were gone, that meant what Jaq was about to reveal was something not for public consumption, but at the same time, it worried Icarus. It could be more bad news.

"No, you don't. Your energy levels are too low. It will take a few days to recover from that kind of deficit without sharing energies, and while I know plenty of single women who'd gladly share with you, I'm pretty sure you aren't ready for that kind of commitment," Jaq said.

Icarus groaned; he knew Jaq was right. It wasn't a simple thing sharing energies. It left a piece of you with whoever you shared energies with, especially in the deep way that would require to help him recover faster.

"At least, tell me if there has been a second attack."

"No, there hasn't been, but that doesn't mean there won't be. Please, rest. We will need you at peak strength when that day comes."

"I feel like I've done enough resting," Icarus protested.

"Being unconscious does not mean you were resting. Since you're in my territory, you are under my rules, okay? Lay your ass down," Tyr said.

Icarus rolled his eyes.

"Fine, but only for today. Anyway, Tyr, the girl who was here before. Was that your Sarah?"

Tyr snorted.

"Yeah, what of it?"

Icarus could feel the fierce protectiveness rolling off of Tyr at the mention of his adopted daughter.

"Don't worry. I just wanted you to know that I am indebted to her. She was the one who brought me back."

Jaq and Tyr exchanged looks.

"What do you mean, she brought you back?"

Icarus was truly confused. Did Tyr know she wasn't just Shifter? Is that why he took her in? Is that why he was so open to helping the Aura? Why would he keep that a secret? Unless, he didn't know, and who knows how he would react if Sarah wasn't the person who told him. Tyr was a trustworthy guy, but lying to your Alpha was a capital offense in Shifter communities.

Jaq crossed the room and placed a hand on Icarus's forehead. Jaq didn't need to do so to see into his head, but with Icarus's weakened state, it was safer. Icarus closed his eyes and didn't fight Jaq's intrusion into his head. A second later, Jaq pulled his hand away, and Icarus opened his eyes.

"Fuck, man," Jaq cursed before turning a worried glance in Tyr's direction.

"Care to explain to me what the fuck is going on?"

Jaq and Icarus exchanged looks. Neither one of them wanted to tell the Alpha Wolf. Jaq may be for Aura liberation and freedom, but he was also about allowing personal choice. Even if the world knew about the Aura, that didn't mean that every Aura had to live openly if they chose not to, and in Sarah's case, it wasn't a stretch to see why she wouldn't want to be open about her Aura ancestry.

Icarus cleared his throat. "Her kindness brought me back. I remember little about when I was unconscious, only that I heard her voice and followed it back."

Tyr seemed to relax with the explanation, but Icarus wasn't entirely fooled by his show of acceptance. Tyr would know he was lying, but thankfully, the Shifter was obviously willing to let it drop for now.

***

Carrie took a deep breath and held it for a moment. She released it with a heavy sigh, letting her shoulders relax. She repeated the cycle three more times before gathering the nerve to knock on the massive doors at the entrance of Kirima's home. Before her hand came in contact with the wood, the door swung open and a servant greeted her.

"The mistress is awaiting you in the parlor."

Carrie forced a smile and nodded.

"Thank you," she said and followed the servant down the hall.

Kirima lounged in a leather chair, sipping a glass of dark liquor. Her posture seemed relaxed, but there was a fire in her eyes, and her hands were clenched tight around her glass.

"What do you want?" she snapped at Carrie.

Carrie nearly turned to run. Kirima was a formidable woman, both in negotiations and on the battlefield. She had earned her spot on the Vampire Council with a trail of blood that almost rivaled that of Maura's. Not for the first time, Carrie began to second-guess herself, but she shook her fears away and straightened her posture.

"I need your help," she said.

Kirima snorted.

"I already have one born Vampire under my protection, I don't have time to baby you as well."

Carrie smiled at the mention of Kirima's daughter. Despite Kirima's brusque nature, Aliridon was quite charming and one of the few born females Carrie considered a friend.

"I'm not here for that. I need your help in taking my father's place on the Council."

"My dear, you are so naïve. The Royals fill that position, your own family, and they have decided Brody is more fitting than you are, even if it's only in a temporary capacity."

"Brody?"

Kirima sat up and turned her full gaze on Carrie. Her eyes were glassy from too much liquor and fiery with barely contained rage.

"You were right about your father's misdeeds. What you were wrong about was the fact that he was working alone."

Carrie sighed.

"Yes, I know my father and the Royal family are backing the Rogues in their trafficking of Aura. I know, and that is why I am here. If we band together, we can stop all of this."

"Two against the entire Vampire aristocracy? I think not. I may have a fearsome reputation, but I am no longer the bloodthirsty bitch they forced me to be."

Kirima sank back into her chair and turned her attention back to her glass. Carrie's head was spinning. This was not the reaction she expected from Kirima. Either way, she needed Kirima's help to end this madness.

"Kirima, I don't care if you're tired. For the sake of Langsmith, for the sake of Aliridon, something must be done. If we roll over now, if we let them continue, the Aura won't be the only ones enslaved by those men. Born females are already kept in gilded cages under constant threat. We can make Langsmith a safe haven. A place where we can all be free to follow our dreams and live in harmony with others."

Kirima took another sip of her drink before setting her glass on a nearby table.

"Alright, alright. We'll give it a shot, but not right now. I need to sober up before dealing with those assholes again."

Carrie couldn't help the smile that came over her features. With Kirima by her side, what could possibly go wrong?

***

"You sure you want to do this?"

Shane massaged Molly's shoulder's as she went over the documents the realtor had sent over the day before. She looked up and smiled at Shane.

"I want to help, and it's the least I can do after the trouble I've caused."

"You sure you're okay with staying here longer?"

"We didn't need that much space anyway, although, I know you were looking forward to the extra room for your lab."

Shane shrugged and bent to place a kiss on her forehead.

"Who knows, maybe I'll get back into teaching. Then I can surely have that space for my lab."

Molly giggled.

"I should hurry so I can get this to Zarovia before going to check on the club."

Shane nodded and kissed her again before disappearing into his tinkering space. The small wing of the mansion they occupied was a little cramped, but giving up her dream house to assist the Aura in starting a school would be well worth it.

Molly tucked the deed into the envelope, along with the papers detailing the transfer of ownership. She could only hope Zarovia was agreeable to the arrangement. Not just Zarovia, but the other Aura. Molly knew they wouldn't trust Vampires so easily, and she hoped Zarovia would understand her intentions. Growing up as a foster child, Molly knew how important it was to feel like you belonged. To have a safe place to just be yourself and not constantly be on-guard.

By doing this she could offer the Aura children a space to do just that, and under the guidance of Zarovia, well, the Aura Academy, as Molly liked to call it, would flourish. Molly made her way out of the mansion and to her car. She was thankful the rain had let up, otherwise, the two hours she spent straightening her hair would have been for not.

The drive into town wasn't too long, but seeing the

ghostly streets put Molly on edge. Langsmith had always felt like a cheerful little town, no matter what the dangers. Families with young children frequented the small shops downtown, and teenagers ran around getting into the usual shenanigans. Yet, there was a marked difference since the night she had defeated Maura. It was as if that one victory had spelled the doom and destruction of everything else around it.

Nothing had gone right since then. Molly laid her hand over the envelope in the passenger seat. It was a time of so much change, and hopefully, with these documents, Molly, for once, would make a completely unselfish difference.

Her car suddenly felt stuffy and stale. She rolled down the window, letting the cool morning air in. The rain had finally stopped, but there was still the icy smell of electricity in the air. Heavy clouds hung low in the sky, threatening to release another torrential downpour. Molly arrived at Zazzie's house and was surprised to see a group of women huddled out front. Molly would have assumed they were customers arriving early for a group reading at Zazzie's shop, except she recognized the women as Aura. More specifically, Zarovia's friends.

She hesitated to get out of the car. She had hoped to just drop off her gift to Zazzie before heading in to check out the club. There was a small leak in the roof that she had meant to get fixed before, and after last night's storm, she hoped it hadn't caused any major damage. Except now, that was a small worry. The women all wore concerned looks as Mack's girlfriend raised her hand to knock on the door, while the wife of the leader of The Resistance made a phone call.

Something wasn't right. She should come back later. Zazzie obviously wasn't home, except where could she be? Molly couldn't help that her curiosity was piqued. She could feel soft tendrils of energy prickling her skin as one woman flared. Then another as a weaker one responded. Molly recognized immediately who the weaker one belonged to, and she jumped out of the car, her gift forgotten on the seat.

***

Red hair and fangs were the last things Zazzie expected to see when she finally opened her eyes.

"Molly?"

The woman shook her head and shrugged out of her jacket, laying it across Zazzie's naked body as Farrah, Disrayan, and Enora skidded to a halt behind her.

"Girl! What the hell?"

Zazzie wanted to know that as well. The last thing she remembered was crying herself to sleep, and then, she'd had the dream again. She reached into herself and felt the burgeoning new energy at her core. The ancestors had returned to her.

"Can I get inside and cleaned up before y'all read me the riot act?"

Disrayan shook her head and trudged toward Zazzie's still open back door. Zarovia could only hope no critters sought shelter in her place while she was out getting scolded and then blessed by the ancestors. Farrah followed Disrayan while Enora joined Molly in helping Zazzie get to her feet. Although Zazzie felt mostly fine, she was utterly exhausted, and her legs felt like jelly. She leaned heavily on both women to get into the house, but mustered enough strength to stand on her own two feet to shrug them both off and head to her bedroom.

There was no reason for Zazzie to look into the mirror in her bathroom. She knew she had to look a hot mess, mud and singed grasses stuck to her skin and filled the gaps beneath her fingernails. Her mouth tasted like

191

copper and feet. Still, with the firing squad waiting in her living room, Zazzie didn't linger in the shower. She got as clean as she could as quickly as she could before meandering out to explain herself.

Farrah had made herself comfortable on the couch, scrolling through messages on her phone and frowning. Disrayan and Enora were making cups of tea in the kitchen. Molly was gone, except there was an extra cup of tea on the counter, so maybe she was outside? As if to answer that question, Molly slid into the room with a thick manila envelope in her hands.

"You need to sit down," Enora said, coming to her side to guide her to the couch next to Farrah.

Disrayan came behind her, carrying the cups of tea on a tray. Molly cautiously joined the group, sitting next to Farrah.

"Speak," Disrayan said as soon as they were all settled.

"Let her at least drink some tea first, Rye," Enora chastised and handed Zazzie a cup of tea.

She even blew on it for good measure. Zazzie couldn't help but smile. Enora had always been the quiet one, but motherly, she was not. Being pregnant had definitely done a number on her.

"Can we hurry this along? She's fine. I've got things to do," Farrah huffed.

Disrayan raised an eyebrow at Farrah before snatching her phone out of her hand.

"As part of the Ruling Council, I decree there is no business more important right now than figuring out what the hell is wrong with Zazzie," Rye said.

"That's not how that works, and you know it," Farrah snapped.

"I don't give a damn. Zazzie is what's important right now. What is more important than making sure our sister is okay?"

Farrah opened her mouth to speak, but Enora stood between them.

"Ladies, can we please stop the bickering?"

"Yes, please. We have company," Zazzie said, letting her eyes fall on Molly. She absorbed the action as if it were a television drama.

"Oh, don't mind me. This is all extremely fascinating."

Disrayan and Farrah both cut looks at Molly before settling back and turning to Zazzie.

"Maybe Farrah is right. We can reconvene at another time," Disrayan said and started to leave, but Zazzie grabbed her arm and pulled her back down into the chair.

"Molly is one of us. She has every right to know what's going on as the rest of us," Zazzie said.

Molly smiled while her friends all looked at her as if she had lost her mind.

"Excuse me?"

"I've been helping Molly learn about the way of the Aura. She is, or was, a lost one before she was turned. Anyway, last night I was in my feelings and the ancestors came to set me straight. Obviously, it didn't go well, but I'm okay, really."

"In your feelings? The ancestors? What happened?" Enora asked.

Zazzie bit her lip and pushed her long locs over her shoulder to keep them out of her face as she spoke.

"Hendrex and I are taking a break from each other."

"A break? Really? Y'all have been on a break for years!" Farrah laughed.

"Why are you so shocked, Farrah? Hendrex is an Andromeda. Y'all love to be all moody and dramatic about your feelings," Disrayan said.

Enora nodded her head in agreement before taking

a sip of her tea.

"So, I take it things haven't been resolved since that Jasmine thing? I mean, a break can be good to bring some perspective to a relationship, as long as you don't wait too long and let old wounds fester instead of heal," Molly asked.

All the women turned their attention to her. Molly's cheeks flamed a bright red, highlighting the sprinkle of freckles across her nose and cheeks.

"Sorry. I don't mean to overstep. I just, well, I have a unique perspective on long relationship breaks," Molly said.

"Right, I hope you don't mind, but Mack told me a little about what happened between you and Shane before you got back together," Disrayan said.

"It's no biggie. I mean, we always loved each other, but sometimes, love just isn't enough. You need to both be in the right place to make a relationship work, and honestly, from what little I know about your situation, I can't see a negative in you two taking time to get things in order before finding your way back to each other," Molly said.

Farrah shook her head.

"Look, what you and Hendrex do is your business. Unless, he really hurts you. Then, I'll kick his ass myself. Anyway, what I saw outside was more than just remnants of a friendly chat with the ancestors. What the hell aren't you telling us, Zazzie?"

Zarovia wasn't sure how to answer. How could she explain? Trying to wrap her head around all of it, would her friends even understand? Was her vision something she was supposed to share? She knew what the ancestors wanted of her, but not how exactly to go about it.

"Earth to Zazzie." Enora waved her hand in front of her face.

Zazzie sat back and sighed.

"I was having a moment, and the ancestors quickly got me together. That's all I can really say about what happened."

Enora bit her lip, Disrayan shook her head, Farrah crossed her arms over her chest, and Molly raised an eyebrow in confusion.

"So, what you're saying is you are on some bull and the Ancestors struck you with lightning? Not just metaphorically, but physically? How the hell are you still standing?"

"If the ancestors spoke to you, they must've given you guidance. I, for one, know what it's like to be given a calling and how scary it can be at first." Enora placed a steadying hand on Zazzie's shoulder. "Just listen to your heart and follow your intuition, that's all the advice I can give."

Farrah smacked her lips. "Y'all are so dramatic."

Disrayan reached over and pinched Farrah's thigh. "I know you are really into the traditions, but don't go messing with visions from the ancestors. That shit is serious. The ancestors sent Mack a vision of the fall of Ceres, and without his help, there wouldn't have been as many survivors as there are."

Molly cleared her throat. "As someone who's been on the other side and has pissed off a few ancestors herself, I can tell you the ancestors are no joke."

Zarovia looked up at Molly, who held her arms and rubbed them as if remembering some great pain rocking her body. One day, Zazzie would ask Molly about her story in detail, but for now, she knew enough to trust the woman.

"I told you what happened. So, why are you all here this morning?"

Farrah and Disrayan quickly filled her in about Icarus

waking and the further drama Jasmine had caused with the Aura. Zazzie could only shake her head as she heard of Jasmine trying to convince the Aura that they needed to cloister together once more. She could understand it, and in a way, her own charge was something similar, only Zazzie didn't want the Aura to hide away any longer. Sure, they needed a safe space that wasn't an old Factory to function out of, but hiding as a people wasn't an option anymore.

"Wow! I didn't know that the Aura were so divided," Molly said.

Zazzie had almost forgotten Molly was there as she had listened to her friends rant about Jasmine.

"Every culture has its issues. It how we deal with them that matters, and right now, we need to figure out a better way," Enora said.

"Yes, I can see that. This must be so hard for you all. I mean, I had my own issues with becoming a Vampire and the whole Maura situation. I know what it's like to feel that the entire world is against you and not knowing where to turn."

Enora placed a hand on Molly's shoulder and smiled.

"But you found your place, and now, you've found us."

Molly blushed and nodded.

"Speaking of belonging, I have something that belongs to you, Zazzie."

Molly grabbed the thick manila envelope she had placed on the coffee table and handed it to Zazzie. She accepted it and carefully peeked inside.

"What is it?"

"The deed to your new property, and hopefully, the future site of the Aura Academy."

Disrayan snatched the envelope from Zazzie's hands and quickly went over the paperwork. Zazzie was too shocked to stop her. She sat there, hands poised as if they still help the envelope, jaw nearly touching the floor.

"Everything looks legit, but you wouldn't mind if I take a closer look before Zazzie agrees to anything?"

Molly nodded.

"No objections from me. I know this is a big gift, but I am giving it with all my heart. I may have found my place now, but I wish I had a place where I could have been myself much sooner. I mean, aside from finding out I was Aura. I was a foster child, and I know what being different can mean in public spaces like schools and things. If I can give even one child a safer place to learn and grow, that would mean the world to me."

There were tears in Molly's eyes. Zazzie's shock wore off, and she moved to give Molly a hug. Soon, all four women were embracing the Vampire. It didn't feel awkward at all. It felt right, and as if to confirm her thoughts, a swell of energy encapsulated the women, their energies not quite merging but harmonizing. Zazzie felt almost invincible, like together they could conquer any and everything that came to pass.

Wheel of Fortune

If there ever was a day for shenanigans, today was the day. Zarovia checked her notebook one last time. Everything was in order, every box was checked, every list she had ever made to get to this point had been completed. With a deep sorrow, she tucked her notebook into her purse and grabbed the keys. The tall building loomed over her, casting a dark, cold shadow, and yet despite this, she felt nothing but joy. Today was the day, today was her day, today was Zenith.

"Welcome to Aura Academy!"

Her happy spirit faltered. Deep inside, she hadn't expected to be alone in for this. She'd expected to have Hendrex by her side, her friends at her back, ready to help her prepare the school for opening, but there she was, all alone. Not even Molly had been able to meet today. Zarovia pressed on, opening the massive door that led into the entryway. Aura Academy was just a pet name for the school. She didn't want to name it something as droll as Langsmith Academy for the gifted, or something as obvious as School of Ceres.

She still had time to decide on a name, though. There was so much that still needed to be done, even if it didn't bode well that she would be so indecisive about such a simple thing. A deceptively simple thing. Nothing about this was simple, nor would it be easy, but it was her life goal. Her calling, her duty.

The estate had been well-kept but was dated. Molly had warned her there would need to be repairs for the place to function as a school. Especially if it would also house students, and possibly faculty and staff. There were more than enough rooms for all of it, but there still had to be some adjustments to the layout.

With a sigh, Zarovia started her tour. Her imagination filled in the reality with her hopes for the future. The entry was large enough for a small receptionist desk to greet parents and students. To the left, there was a guest parlor that could work as her office, or a small conference room to meet with parents and prospective students.

Farther down the hall, a grand ballroom that could function as the cafeteria or an assembly hall. While Zazzie was somewhat familiar with the requirements needed for a functioning learning space, she would still need help from Disrayan in settling all the legal matters involved. Why she hadn't thought of that sooner baffled her. She pulled out her phone and called Rye.

"How is the building?"

Zazzie smiled.

"It's amazing. How are things going at the Factory?"

Disrayan snorted.

"Chaos. Jasmine is really making things harder than they need to be. Icarus is in hot water because he is being blamed for the attack. Jaq is with Enora for her appointment, of course. I wish I could see the building with you today, instead of dealing with all of this."

"It's okay, there will be plenty of opportunity for that later. I hate to add to your burden, but I could really use your help with legally establishing the school."

"I was wondering when you would ask. I already

have a packet of information for you and paperwork to sign."

Zazzie sighed with relief.

"Thank you, Rye."

"Don't thank me yet. Just wait until you see how much paperwork it is. Besides, establishing the school to the human world is the easy part. It's the Aura you will have the most trouble convincing. Especially now with Jasmine in everyone's head about secluding ourselves."

"Forget Jasmine. We need this school. I am going to make it happen. The ancestors have demanded it."

"The ancestors also led us here."

"Which is why they are helping us now to right the wrongs of the past."

"Are they truly?"

"Yes, I believe so."

"Well, since you are the spiritual goddess among us, I will have to take your word on that."

There was a commotion in the background on Disrayan's end of the line. Frantic, angry voices gave Zazzie a chill down her spine.

"I'll let you go now, Rye, I'll be by this afternoon for the paperwork."

"Yeah, yeah. I gotta go," Disrayan hung up quickly, and Zazzie gazed up at the vaulted ceilings.

She could understand Disrayan's doubt of the ancestors. It was easy to discredit them in times of strife, but Zarovia needed to hold on to her faith.

At this point, it was almost all she had left. Just as Zazzie put her phone away, it buzzed. She resisted the urge to ignore it. Something told her it probably had to do with whatever had rushed Disrayan off the line.

Sure enough, there was a message from Farrah in the group text.

F: Donovan has requested us at the shifter compound,

he didn't give an explanation.

E: Jaq texted me as well. Super vague. I hate when the boys get all cagey. Just grabbed Disrayan, we are on our way.

Zazzie shook her head. Taking one last look at the building, she stepped back through the doors and headed to the Shifter compound on the other side of the mountain.

***

Hendrex shifted on the couch. It wasn't the most comfortable place to sleep, but it was better than the floor. The floor at the Factory was filthy, covered in dirt and dust after months of neglect. Hendrex wasn't complaining. He was lucky to have found the small corner. The small space, out of the way of the hustle and bustle, held an old couch that was just barely big enough to fit him. That seemed to be the way his life was going now after the fall. Making himself small, making himself fit where others wanted him to.

Mack had offered for Hendrex to stay with him and Disrayan. But that would not happen. Staying on their couch meant a good chance of running into Zazzie. Right now, Hendrex couldn't face her. He really needed to change that. He needed to find his way as a man in his new reality. Then and only then would he be able to plead his case with Zazzie. To make her see that he was worthy of her affection.

Hendrex sat up and rubbed his face. The stubble on his cheeks scratched the palms of his hands. He reached over to his bag to grab a razor but thought better of it. Maybe Mack had had the right idea by leaving. Maybe Hendrex needed to go on his own soul-searching trip before jumping in to things with Zarovia. If he wasn't acting as Magistrate, he would have left already. His phone buzzed, nearly falling off the arm of the couch. Hendrex caught it in time to see Jaq's name on the screen. He would call his cousin back later. He dragged himself off the couch and headed to his office. Disrayan had left some paperwork on his desk involving the school Zazzie wanted to open.

Another reason for him to give Zazzie space. She would be too busy getting the school running to have time to date or court her properly. Even though Hendrex had been elected Magistrate, there were those in the Aura community who didn't trust him. Who didn't trust his motives and looked down on anyone who did trust him. Which was the last thing Zazzie needed to be tied to when trying to gain their trust to help their children. So, he would support her as Magistrate, but personally, their relationship would have to wait.

Hendrex started shuffling papers across his desk when his office door opened and his cousin Farrah strode in. He and Farrah hadn't always been on the best of terms. After everything with Zarovia, he didn't expect that to change. She stopped in front of his desk, propping her hip on the edge. She sucked her teeth.

"What bullshit am I hearing about you and Zazzie taking a break?"

"Farrah, I don't have time for this."

"Oh, you're going to make time for this. Should be making time to apologize to Zazzie."

Hendrex shook his head.

"This doesn't involve you, Farrah. Now, if you don't have any official business," he gestured toward the door.

Farrah snatched paperwork out of his hands and slammed it on the desk.

"I'm going to need you and the other Andromeda men to get your heads out of your asses. You are giving us a bad name. Y'all play too much."

"I'm not playing at anything. Now just isn't the time for a relationship. I don't even know if there was a relationship."

Farrah stuck her finger in his face.

"Don't be like your brother. Don't make obstacles where there are none. You have loved Zazzie for as long as I can remember, and as far as I can tell, she feels the same. Now, I get that love isn't everything. But it can be if you let it. So, if you really want her, find the courage and don't be a big, dumb baby about it. Find Zazzie and have the talk that y'all need to have."

"Is that all?"

His cousin was correct. He wasn't going to tell her that, though. So instead, he kept his face aloof and reached for the documents taken from him.

"No, that isn't all. I want to know where you, Mack, Jaq, and my fiancé have been slipping off to."

That made Hendrex chuckle. He definitely wasn't going to tell her that.

"Why don't you go ask your fiancé? Or better yet, your brother?"

"Don't think I didn't start there. I know you're more tight-lipped than a 100-year-old can of Spam."

"I have no idea what that means. I'm just going to guess that means you already know I'm not going to tell you, so why did you bother asking?"

Farrah eased off of his desk and sank to the rickety chair across from it. For the first time, Hendrex noticed the worry lines creasing her forehead. They may not always get along, but Farrah was family, and he hated to see her stressed.

"I'm just done with all the secrets."

Hendrex sat back. "I am too."

The somber mood in the room could have suffocated an ant. It didn't last long as Jaq barged into the room.

"Man, why you answering your phone?"

"Why? Something happened?"

"We've got to roll," Jaq said.

Farrah cleared her throat. "Where we going?"

Jaq spun around, finally noticing Farrah in the room.

"Not you. Don't you have a Binding to plan?"

Farrah stood and got in her brother's face.

"I'm about tired of your attitude. I'm not just for backup."

"That's something to discuss with your man, not me."

Hendrex smirked at the siblings' display. Even though their words were harsh, he could see the humor glinting in their eyes. He had always envied Farrah and Jaq's dynamic. He and Mack were twins, but they had never shared this level of camaraderie. That was changing now, but it was a shame it was something he still needed to work on.

Further evidence that he was the issue. All of his problems came back to his inability to have a healthy, genuine relationship. He didn't know how to be himself without the pressures of upholding his family name, representing his people, and being a role model. How could he give Zazzie something he didn't have?

"Are we just going to stand here all day? Let's just go," Hendrex said.

Hendrex got up from his chair and grabbed his coat. He didn't wait for them to answer. If he waited for any sort of confirmation from those two, they would really be there all day. Once Farrah and Jaq got started, it was hard for them to stop. Whatever had happened must have been important for Jaq to come in person to get him.

The trio made their way through the Factory, passing the rows of families still present after the fall of Ceres. They did their best not to let the urgency of their exit show. There was no need to alarm the families any further. They were almost to the parking lot when Jasmine stepped into their path.

"What's going on?"

Farrah stepped close to Jasmine, just shy of being within a disrespectful distance. Part of Hendrex wanted to pull Farrah back. But at the same time, he was tired of Jasmine's interference. He could understand her motives. He understood that Jasmine was doing what she felt was right, but how could she make such decisions when she refused to look at the other side?

"Get out of the way, Jasmine," Farrah said.

Jasmine glared at Farrah. Raising her chin to look down at her, using her significant height advantage.

"You will address me as Ruling One, Miss Andromeda."

Farrah rolled her eyes. "I didn't vote for your ass. I wouldn't address you at all if you weren't so keen on getting in my goddamn way all the time."

Hendrex winced. He knew Farrah was in a bad mood, but this was heated, even for her. He looked at Jaq for help, but the smug smile on Jaq's face told him not to bother.

"Ladies, this is not the time. Jasmine, you're welcome to come with us. I think it would be best for all of us if we were as transparent as possible."

There was a tense few minutes as Farrah and Jasmine continued to stare each other down.

"Let's just let these two go at it," said Jaq.

He walked away toward his car, and Hendrex followed. He didn't expect the women to join, but both slid into the backseat of Jaq's SUV.

"I'm only coming to ensure you no longer endanger the Aura with rash decisions," Jasmine said.

Hendrex shook his head. He did not know what

was happening or what he was walking into, but having Jasmine there would undoubtedly make things much more complicated.

***

Sarah paced around her room. She held her phone in her hand, moving it from one hand to the other. It was almost time. Any minute now, Tyr and Sequoia would stop whispering in their bedroom and come to her. The anticipation was killing her. It would have been easier if they had done this the day Icarus had woken, but Tyr had dragged it out a whole day just to torture her. What would she say? What would this mean for her standing in the pack?

She didn't doubt that Tyr and Sequoia would always care for her as their own, but the revelation of her being part Aura really threw a wrench in things. Sarah's phone buzzed in her hands with a text from Keenan.

K: did you talk to them yet?

S: not yet, still waiting

K: it's going to be okay. No matter what happens you always got me in the crew.

S: thank you, I know. How are things on your end?

K: same old same old. Matt, on his trip in, called my sister.

Sarah chuckled. Keenan had told her stories about his older sister Akellah. If his Aunt had called her in, things were serious.

S: is she coming to straighten you out?

K: Yeah, she's coming, but I don't need any straightening.

S: you sure about that?

K: I'm straight as an arrow.

He added an eggplant emoji for emphasis. Sarah rolled her eyes.

S: you're gross.

K: real talk, though. I know what I am doing and what I want out of life.

S: That doesn't mean you don't still need your ass checked every once in a while.

K: that's what I have you and Daphne for.

Sarah picked up on the sound of footsteps approaching.

S: damn straight, but family is important too. Anyway, the time has come. I'll text you later.

Sarah tossed her phone onto her side table before flopping down on her bed. She was already exhausted, and the interrogation hadn't even started yet. What if Tyr wasn't as understanding as she thought? What if he saw this as an opportunity for advancement in the Shifter ranks? He was ambitious, after all.

There was a soft knock on her bedroom door, Sequoia.

"Come in!"

To Sarah's surprise, it was only Sequoia who entered. Her heart sank a little. Tyr would only be absent for this talk if he wasn't okay with what he knew she had to say.

Coy sat on the edge of Sarah's bed and sighed.

"Start talking, young lady."

Sarah sat up and crossed her legs.

"I am part Aura. I didn't know it until the night Ceres fell."

Coy nodded.

"Okay, but why didn't you tell us? I know what it's like trying to figure out two competing cultures at once. Tyr has always had your back, and the fact that you hid this from him…"

Coy looked genuinely hurt, and Sarah started to understand how upset Tyr must be. Sarah felt even worse.

"I… I honestly didn't know what to do. You and Tyr

were dealing with a lot already, and it is not like I didn't plan to tell you both at some point."

"And that's okay, Sarah. It really is. I didn't come here to guilt you. I am sorry. Tyr and I just want you to know that we are here for you. No matter where this new information takes you, we are here for you. We just ask that you don't hide things like this from us. We took on the responsibility of being your parents; you agreed to let us do that. For the love of all things holy, let us parent you."

And there it was. The reason Tyr really hadn't come to this discussion. He promised her when he took her in that she would always be on equal footing. It was a partnership, but that had changed when Coy came into the picture. Tyr understood her need for independence. Her need to be her own person, even if she was under his protection. Coy, on the other hand, had been raised human, and her ideas on parenting were uncomfortable to Sarah. She'd gotten a bit more used to it, but still the whole idea of real parents gave Sarah the hives.

Coy must have insisted on bringing up this whole parenting thing. Which meant Tyr would probably have his own talk with Sarah later. Sarah groaned and turned away from Sequoia.

"I really appreciate all you and Tyr have done for me, but you have to understand, I can't do parents. I can't be parented."

Coy sighed.

"I think the issue here isn't being parented, but you not knowing what real parenting is supposed to be. It breaks my heart, but I will concede to not using the p-word in the future. However, I will call it caring because that's what it is. I care about you, Tyr cares about you. Let us care about you and guide you when you are feeling lost."

When she put it that way, Sarah felt much better

about the idea.

"Okay. I promise to do my best to be more open about things."

"Thank you," Coy smiled.

Sarah smiled back, and to show that she was truly committed to the idea, she pulled Sequoia into a hug. It was brief, but still a hug Sarah had initiated, which was rare and would mean the world to Coy.

Coy quickly wiped tears from her eyes and laughed when Sarah pulled away.

"Now, Tyr asked me to discuss one more thing with you."

Sarah frowned.

"What?"

"Energy sharing? I don't know entirely what that means, but the way Tyr talked about it, apparently its more intimate than sex for the Aura."

That wasn't entirely news to Sarah, but it still made her cringe. The Shifter community was not shy about mating and all it entailed, but they ran on instinct. If your gut felt it was okay, it was. Humans and Aura were different, and somehow that made this conversation much more cringeworthy than the brief discussion she had with Tyr the first time a Shifter male had made eyes at her.

"It can be intimate, but I promise I haven't shared energy like that with anyone. Like, there are levels to it. I've mostly done energy sharing for healing purposes."

"Still, you need to be careful. We wouldn't want any misunderstandings. Sharing energy like that connects you with the person, much like the Shifter mating bond. A piece of you is left behind with them, and vice versa."

Sarah bit her lip.

"I promise to be careful."

"Good, now that we've had that talk, I can tell you

that Tyr is waiting for you in the Meeting House. I will walk with you."

"That serious?"

Coy shrugged.

"He didn't tell me, and I honestly stay out of all the politics. I mated Tyr because I love him. His pack status was actually a negative for me. I do what I must, but otherwise, I like to keep to myself."

"Alright, alright. Let's head over."

***

The first thing Zazzie noticed when she walked in the room was that there was a shit ton of people there. Farrah had informed her via text that she needed to get to the Shifter compound immediately. For the life of her, Zazzie didn't know why. She was guided into the Meeting Room. On one side was Tyr, Sequoia, and Sarah. On the other side of the room was everyone else. Farrah, Donovan, Jaq, Enora, Mack, Hendrex, Icarus, Disrayan, and Jasmine all stood in an awkward little huddle.

Everyone turned their attention to her as she entered. Sarah mouthed "sorry" while Tyr gave her a grim look.

"Guess I'm late to the party," Zazzie tried to make light of the situation.

"We're all here to find out what's going on."

Zarovia nodded and joined her friends in the row of chairs that had been moved from around the large round table that had been shoved into a corner. While everyone else was seated, Tyr stood with Sarah at the long wall that held what looked to be an old chalkboard. For a moment, Zazzie wondered if this room was the round table Meeting Room she overheard Hendrex mention once in a hushed call with his brother. Men and their not-so-secret meetings.

"Sarah tells us you have been training her in her

210

Aura abilities." Tyr addressed her.

That's what this was all about. Sarah had finally told Tyr, or rather, he found out about her being an Aura. It was a relief. At least, a small one. This she could handle. Had prepared for it when Sarah was ready to tell him, she'd known he would come to her for answers. What she hadn't expected was the audience. She had supposed it would be a more intimate conversation, private. Like a parent teacher conference or something.

"Yes, Sarah and a few others, who need guidance, came to me. I wasn't going to turn them away."

"Did it not occur to you to get permission?" Jasmine snapped.

Zazzie took a deep breath and turned to face Jasmine. She made a silent plea for strength before opening her mouth to speak directly to the woman.

"I obtained permission to work with the students after school. I just didn't specify what we would be working on. Review of my lesson plans was not included in the agreement signed by the Council before the fall, nor was it part of the existing agreement."

Jasmine wasn't as good at keeping her emotions off her face or out of her tone. Years of being part of the shelter of Ceres meant she'd never had to learn the way women of color were taught to contain themselves for the comfort of others. In some ways, Zazzie envied that, while on the other hand, it made their interaction that much more contentious.

"This is exactly the type of behavior that got us in this mess in the first place. People working for their own goals and not the betterment of the whole."

What Zazzie would have given to throw something at Jasmine right then. Except there were three people between them, and Zazzie had already shown Jasmine what happened when she crosses the line. Here was not the time or place to start an argument with the woman. Let alone, teach her yet another lesson in bitch, don't try me. Right now, the focus was obviously on Sarah and whatever she had done to out herself before she was ready.

"I will apologize for not being transparent, but it was Sarah's choice whether it was known she is Aura or not."

Tyr sighed. He obviously didn't want to deal with the internal drama of the Aura on top of everything else.

"I want you to continue training Sarah. I don't fully understand the whole energy thing, but I've seen what can happen when it's not under control. We've all seen it. I'm not here to get into your business, I'm solely here as a concerned parent."

Zazzie raised an eyebrow at him. If it was truly just about being a concerned parent, there was no need for this massive audience of people.

"What Tyr is trying to say is that we brought you here for guidance," added Sequoia.

That made a little more sense to Zazzie, but not really. As far as she knew, none of the others knew about Sarah's abilities until now. No one aside from herself and Jasmine had any experience in teaching young Aura. Well, maybe Jaq, but if he were effective at it, half his little resistance Army wouldn't beg to be in her classes with Sarah and Daphne.

"I will gladly continue training Sarah if you are okay with it," said Zazzie.

Jasmine scoffed and crossed her arms over her chest.

"This unofficial school of yours is not sanctioned by the Ruling Council. If you want true guidance in the way of the Aura, Sarah will have to be fostered by an Aura family. Maybe if we find her real family, they will take her in."

The tension in the room ratcheted up by half. It

had already been nearly stifling to begin with. Who had invited Jasmine anyway? She was doing nothing but making things worse for everyone involved.

"Sarah is with her true family," growled Tyr.

Alpha energy rolled off Tyr, feeling like hot embers falling over everything. If someone didn't calm the situation soon, Jasmine would likely ruin the truce the Aura had with Tyr and the Langsmith pack.

Jaq stood up and crossed the room, putting himself between Tyr and Jasmine.

"Don't mind her. She doesn't speak for the whole Council."

While everyone else's focus was on Jasmine and Tyr, Zazzie watched Sarah. Watched how she tensed, a rare flash of fear crossing her face before her eyes clouded up with the impending storm of her own anger. Sarah's own Alpha energy coalescing around her.

"It doesn't matter, anyway. No matter what you say, I will always be Shifter first," Sarah spoke.

Sequoia placed a hand on Sarah's shoulder. The other woman's presence calmed Sarah enough that the massive energy explosion Sarah had brewing didn't come.

"We know, Sarah. But maybe Jasmine has a point. Not saying that you should go and live with the Aura, but maybe finding your lineage could be good for you."

Zazzie winced. That was not the right approach to this situation, even if what Sequoia said was true. Sarah shook her head and ran out of the room. Tyr shot his mate an angry look, and Sequoia threw her hands up in the air and left in a huff after the girl.

"We have other business to discuss, but I want that one off the compound right now," Tyr said, pointing at Jasmine.

Icarus looked around the room waiting for anyone

to protest Tyr's decree, but none came. He shook his head in obvious disappointment. Icarus might not be the most traditional Aura, but he was loyal to the Aura above all others. That meant he wasn't at all okay with the way they were willing to throw Jasmine under the bus in favor of the shifters. If it were any other person Zazzie may have stepped in and said something but not for Jasmine. Not after all the shit she had pulled over the last few weeks.

"Come on, Jasmine, let's go back to the Factory. We need to prepare to present this to our people, anyway." Icarus said.

Once they left, everyone got to work shifting the room around so that the round table was at the center of the room with the chairs circling it. Everyone paired up with their respective partners, but Hendrex made a beeline for the seat beside Tyr, the furthest he could get from Zazzie. When he sat, he avoided her gaze. It was painfully clear the lengths that Hendrex would go to avoid her. It hurt. Was this how it was going to be? Would he always be this stiff and cold around her? There really wasn't a reason for her to stay. Although, she helped with some of the mission, for the most part, Zazzie was usually just there for backup, then take an active part in the planning and politics. She didn't have to put up with this slight. His lack of interest in her and the obvious tension it caused.

"I think I'll help Sequoia look for Sarah."

Zarovia left before anyone could stop her.

***

Five stories up in the Vampire Council's regional office building, Kirima and Carrie stood in front of the male members of the Vampire Council as they laughed in their faces. More specifically, Brody and Nathaniel.

214

The other two at least contained their laughter to giggles behind the shield of their hands. The ring of thrones once seemed decadent and imposing, but the more Carrie learned, the less magnificent it all seemed. The men before her were merely pawns. There was no real power here, just gaudy furniture tied to a useless title and an extreme amount of ego.

"You want us to cease taking advantage of our most profitable natural resource because it's not nice?" Nathaniel balked.

"This isn't even your region of influence," Carrie spat.

Nathaniel stood and got in her face.

"Listen, little girl, you have no idea of what you speak. Why don't you be a good little girl and get married? You need a good man to squash those flighty ideas you've come up with."

Brody stepped forward. "If it's a man you need, I'd be happy to step in."

Carrie saw red, and not just through her own anger, but because in two swift blows, both Nathaniel and Brody were headless. There hadn't been guards present, since it was a closed meeting of the Council. The other two Council members cowered behind their chairs. Carrie turned slowly to Kirima. Kirima's clothing was mostly unscathed, aside from a few splotches here and there, but her blade was coated with red. Carrie hadn't even known Kirima brought a sword with her.

"You two have anything more to add?" Kirima taunted the others.

The twins shook their heads in the negative.

"No, Kirima, we're good."

Kirima smiled, flashing her elongated canines in a show of dominance.

"Then run along. This matter no longer concerns

you, and from this point on, you must submit to me for approval to step foot in Langsmith, understand?"

The twins nodded furiously before taking off. Carrie hadn't realized she held her breath until they were gone, and it seemed the Council guards had deemed it their prerogative to let the chips fall where they may before deciding who was worthy of their protection. Even with it being a closed meeting, they wouldn't have been so far as not to have heard the commotion and come running. Another blow to the safety and security Carrie had felt in her status and the protections it had provided her in the past. Kirima lifted her blade to her lips and licked one side of it clean before offering it to Carrie.

"It's tradition to consume the blood of your enemies," she said.

Carrie cringed.

"Can we change tradition? I mean, Langsmith is ours now, right? We don't have to live by their rules."

Kirima shook her head and pressed the blade to Carrie's lips.

Carrie reluctantly let the blood enter her mouth. Warmth spread through her mouth before shooting into her body. She felt powerful and arrogant, like nothing in the world could touch her. Then the visions began. Not visions, per se, but brief flashes of memory. Not hers, but Brody's and Nathaniel's. Talks with Merwin and Cain, run-ins with other creatures not quite Vampires, not quite Shifters.

"What the hell?" a female voice said from behind them. Kirima and Carrie turned around, Kirima held her blade ready to fight and the woman who spoke also held a weapon. A male rushed in, fangs bared and eyes as black as sin.

"Who are you?" Carrie asked.

The woman lowered her weapon. The male beside

her growled in protest, but she held up her hand and he, too, calmed. His fangs receded, and the black in his eyes receded to a deep amber gaze.

"You're Carolina, daughter of Maximus, and you are Kirima the Bloodletter," the woman said as if in awe of Kirima, not Carrie.

"That doesn't answer my question," Kirima said. Carrie put her arm up as if it would prevent Kirima from anything.

"I'm Akellah, and this is my partner Hectair."

The man beside her looked pained by her words.

"Mate, love. The correct term is mate," he said.

Akellah shot him a glare before turning her attention back to Carrie and Kirima.

"Look, I'm just a human girl in the know, looking for some answers."

Carrie made a face. How could an Aura think she was human? Maybe she didn't know they knew about the Aura. Carrie put on her friendliest smile.

"Why don't we find a safer place than this to chat? I'm sure we both have a lot to talk about."

"Where do you suggest we go?"

Carrie looked around the room before pulling out her phone. She dialed Greg's number.

"Where are you?" she asked when he answered.

"Shifter compound, there's some stuff going down. I'll fill you in later."

"No need, I'll come there and hear it firsthand."

Carrie hung up before Greg could protest.

"We're headed to the Shifter compound!"

***

Hendrex felt like an ass. He wished Zarovia had stayed. He didn't blame her for leaving, while at the same time, any chance to see her and be in her presence

217

was precious to him. On top of that, everyone gave him accusatory looks.

"Bro, you need to fix that."

Mack shook his head.

"Let's just get this business over with so I can," Hendrex said.

Everyone nodded in agreement.

"I know it's only been a few days, but we really need to decide what we're going to do about the Vampire problem."

"At this point, I think we should change our focus. We've been on the defense, now we need to focus on offense."

"I don't think provoking them further is going to help," said Disrayan.

"I don't either, but I don't think we have a choice," said Donovan.

"So, how are we going to do this, and are we going to involve Maura's Men, as well?"

There was silence around the room as everyone considered the options. On one hand, having some Vampires on their side could be beneficial. What better way to know thy enemy than to befriend them? On the other hand, if there was any chance of a truce, being friendly with Maura's Men would put them at a disadvantage.

"I don't think we should turn our backs on our friends," Mack said.

Hendrex and Mack exchanged looks. At least on this, they were on the same page.

"I agree. We need their expertise," Hendrex said.

"Yes, we do, but can we trust them? There is a reason they are cast out of their own society," Tyr said.

"I think because they are outcast, we can trust them," said Enora.

"Then I think we should get them here so we can start making plans."

Mack pulled out his cell phone and, a minute later, announced Maura's Men would arrive soon.

"While we wait, I think I'll go find Zazzie," Hendrex said.

Farrah smirked and kicked him under the table.

"Yeah, you go do that," she snapped.

Hendrex didn't have to be told twice. He stood and left the room, heading into the open air. He carefully let energy slip out and search for Zarovia. He didn't want to wander too far out on the compound, but thankfully, neither had Zazzie. She sat on the front porch of Tyr's cabin talking to Sequoia. The women were smiling and laughing, and for a moment, Hendrex stood by and watched.

He noted the brightness of Zazzie's tone and the radiance of her skin, but he could tell something was off. She seemed tired, and her laughter didn't ring entirely true. Hendrex hated the thought that he caused it. He approached the women, and their conversation stopped. Sequoia stood and brushed off her jeans.

"I'll let you two talk."

Zazzie looked as if she would protest, but Sequoia was already at the door and gone. Zazzie turned to Hendrex, fire in her eyes. "What do you want?"

"We need to talk."

"Do we?"

"Yes, there is a lot we need to discuss."

"Honestly, I'm not sure that I care at this point."

Zazzie stood and stomped off toward the Meeting Room. Hendrex grabbed her arm as she passed. The moment his fingertips came in contact with her skin, he received a jolt of energy so strong he nearly blacked out. When his vision returned, he was cradled in her arms.

She supported him as he was literally almost prone to the ground.

"What the hell was that?"

Zazzie looked sheepish.

"The ancestors paid me a visit and now my energy is heightened," she admitted.

As much as Hendrex would have loved to continue on that line of conversation, he didn't want to get sidetracked. They had little time before he would have to go back into the meeting.

"I'll ask about that later, but right now, I think I should get to the point. Zazzie, I love you."

Zazzie rolled her eyes. "Wow, you're a bigger asshole than I thought."

She let him fall to the dirt and stood up. Hendrex scrambled to his feet.

"So, you don't feel the same? You don't dream of me at night the way I dream of you? You don't catch the lingering scent of me on your clothes and smile like I do? You don't wish that you could wake up to my face every morning?"

She kept her back to him, but at least, she didn't walk away.

"All of those things sound nice. But we had all those nice things, and you walked away."

He wrapped his arms around her and rested his head on her shoulder.

"I didn't intend for it to be me walking away. You packed up my things. You asked for space. I just wanted to be a man worth your time."

"And that's why I felt we needed space. I'm not in the habit of wasting my time. If I didn't think you are worth it, we wouldn't have gotten to the place we were at."

Zazzie turned to face him.

"What are you trying to do here?"

"Zazzie, I want to be with you. I want to love you and cherish you for the rest of our lives. All I ask is that you give me time to be the man I need to be for you."

"I think you mean, the man you need to be for you. I can understand that. I appreciate the sentiment, but your actions with Jasmine, your actions in the face of any real conflict between us, have shown me otherwise."

"I know, which is why I'm trying to clear this up now before it's too late. It's not too late, is it?"

Zazzie didn't answer. She looked everywhere but directly at him. Hendrex knew he needed to do more, to show he was serious about this, about her, about them. Hendrex sank to his knees and pulled her to him. Resting his head on her midsection, he held her tight.

"Zarovia, my love, my goddess. Please give me another chance."

Never in his life did he imagine he would beg a woman for her affection, but if for any woman, it would be for Zazzie.

"Get up, Hendrex."

"Not until you answer me. Is it too late?"

He had her attention now. Her brown eyes glistened with tears. She grabbed him by the collar and pulled him up until their lips touched. A slight brush of her lips over his, but it filled his body with heat and need he couldn't deny.

"No, it's not too late."

Hendrex smiled, and Zazzie smiled back. He leaned in for a real kiss when they were interrupted by a shout from behind.

"Oh my God, the Shifter compound is actually as I thought it would look!"

Hendrex turned to see Xander, Claude, Shane, and their mates, coming from the entrance of the compound.

Zazzie pulled away from him and waved at the group.

"Hey, guys! What are you doing here?" she called and headed toward the group.

He wasn't going to let her go so easily. He pulled her back to him, her luscious curves aligning perfectly with his body.

"They know where they are going," he whispered in her ear before pulling her out of the main clearing and into the brush.

He wanted privacy for what he planned to do next.

***

"Hendrex," Zazzie gasped as he teased the sensitive spot on her neck with his tongue.

She had no idea what had come over him, but she also had no intention of stopping him. Especially, as he pulled her jeans down her hips enough to bury his hands between her thighs. She gripped his shoulders, leaning against a nearby tree for support as her legs became jelly.

He pressed her back against the thick tree trunk. The rough bark scratched at her back as he lifted her off the ground.

"Wrap your legs around me," he said.

She did just that. His hand sandwiched between their two bodies, rubbing roughly against her clit, her inner muscles gripping thick fingers tightly. They felt amazing inside of her, but as she closed her eyes, her imagination took over, imagining his fingers as a much larger and thicker part of his anatomy. An orgasm tore through her, and she leaned forward to kiss Hendrex. She screamed her release into his mouth.

Hendrex slid his fingers from her core and let her legs drop to the ground. He pulled her pants to her ankles, following their path until he was on his knees before her. She knew what he was about to do, but she wanted more.

"Hendrex," she breathed as he buried his face between her legs.

"Yes, love?"

"As much as I love what you're able to do with your mouth, I need more."

Hendrex dragged his tongue across her slit and moaned.

"So do I."

Before she could process his words, he spun her around and bent her over. She gripped the tree to keep herself steady as he pressed his face against her from behind. This wasn't what she meant, but Hendrex was very good with his tongue, and as her second orgasm ripped into her, she could hardly complain. She started to stand, but Hendrex pressed his palm firmly on her lower back, keeping her in place.

"We should—" Her words were cut off as she felt the hot bulb of him teasing the entrance to her vagina.

Hendrex leaned over her back and pressed soft kisses along her shoulders and neck as he slid inside.

"You're mine, Zarovia, now and forever."

He held himself deep inside of her, rubbing his hips in a circular motion until the head of him found just the right spot, and Zazzie cried out.

"Fuck!"

"Is this where you want me, baby?"

Zazzie nodded enthusiastically as he made short strokes in and out, teasing the spot with every inward thrust. As good as he felt, she wanted to see his face, wanted to watch him enjoying her. She stepped out of her pants and pulled away from him. Hendrex hissed as he slid out of her. His hands gripped her hips as he tried to pull her back into position, but she was determined. She grabbed his collar and pulled him closer to the tree. She wrapped a leg around his waist and gripped his dick.

He was slick with her arousal, and she guided him back to her core. She smiled as his eyes fluttered closed, and his face twisted in pure ecstasy.

"Fuck, Zazzie," he groaned. She squeezed her inner muscles, drawing out his pleasure as much as she did her own.

"Come for me, Hendrex," she whispered in her ear.

With a growl, he picked up the pace of his strokes, his hips slapping against her inner thighs with a satisfying smack. There was not one ounce of control to his movements, and knowing she could break his carefully constructed control was sexy as hell. He stilled, pressed fully inside of her. She could feel him pulsing with his own orgasm, and she could no longer stop the freight train that was her own release.

***

The room was tense when Zazzie and Hendrex entered the meeting. They almost didn't notice in the after-sex high they were on. Their good mood was immediately squashed at the sight of two Vampire women in the room.

"Good, now that we are all here, we can get this started," Mack said.

"Who are our new guests?" Hendrex asked.

"I am Kirima, a former member of the Vampire Council," the larger of the two women said.

Hendrex hadn't been aware of any Vampire females in power. He'd assumed that was squashed after the rise of Maura. Apparently not.

"And I'm Carrie. Nice to finally meet you all. Greg has told me how nice you are. I know you've had trouble with the Vampires of Langsmith, and that's why Kirima and I are here. We are now in charge of Langsmith and have declared it a protected area outside of the jurisdiction of the Royal family."

"Outside their jurisdiction?" Xander said, gaping at Kirima and Carrie.

"As you know, my father was behind the kidnapping of Aura in the area, but he wasn't the mastermind of it all. He was working on behalf of the Royal family, or rather one member of the Royal family. I can't say for certain that everyone in the Royal Court was aware of the happenings here, but that doesn't mean they aren't also complicit."

"I'm confused. There are Royal Vampires?" Enora said.

"It's a long story, but to be more concise, Royal Vampires are the original line. Every Vampire descends from the Royal family line. Anyway, all that matters is now more than ever, we need to work together to ensure the safety of Langsmith. The Royal family won't give up easily," Carrie explained.

"What about the rest of the Vampire Council?"

"We've handled them," Kirima said.

Hendrex did not like the tone of the woman's voice when she spoke.

"How exactly, if you don't mind me asking?"

"Two are dead. The other two chose to bow out gracefully."

Xander cursed in the corner.

"The Royal Vamps aren't going to just let this happen, if they are behind the trafficking. They will expect to keep that going no matter what you have declared."

"I have some help with that." Carrie waved toward the door. Everyone turned to see a young woman and a massive male with long flowing hair behind them.

"Hey cousin, long time no see," the young woman said.

"Akellah?" Enora said.

Enora stood and rushed to the woman, giving her a big hug. Hendrex leaned over to Zazzie.

"I thought Enora didn't have any living family?"

Zazzie nudged him and shook her head.

After letting the women chat between themselves for a moment, Tyr cleared his throat. Hendrex could tell the Alpha Shifter was already on edge with the Vampire Council present, but his eyes were glued firmly on Akellah's companion.

"And you are?" Tyr asked, his voice low and menacing.

The man stepped forward and smiled, revealing large sharp fangs, closer to a Shifter's fangs than a Vampire, but a sustained partial shift wasn't something Hendrex had ever seen before. Curious, he reached out with his energy. The man's energy read like nothing Hendrex had ever encountered before. Shifters were dual spirited but their energy was one at their core just like the Aura's. This man had two separate energies running through him, one similar to that of a shifter's energy the other more akin to a Vampire only not dead. The energy was darker, more menacing and very much alive, just nothing like anything of this earth. Hendrex stood and shook his head.

"What are you?" he blurted before he could catch himself.

"My name is Hectair, and I'm here to offer you the truth about your so-called Royal Vampires."

"Leave it to the Omri to beat around the bush, we ain't Royalty. We're not from this world," another voice said before a tall man stepped forward seemingly out of nowhere.

Akellah drew a gun from somewhere and trained it directly at the newcomer. Hectair growled low in his throat. Even Kirima reached for her sword. The rest of the room either stood still locked in by the spectacle before them or positioned themselves to trap the newcomer if necessary.

"Cain," Kirima said, her voice laced with deadly calm.

Cain smirked and scanned the room. "I was sent by Merwin to squash whatever rebellion was happening here but Merwin is out of his ever-loving mind. I've been observing you all for the last week and have decided I'd like to help you."

Hectair cocked his head to the side in question but didn't relax his battle-ready stance.

"And you expect me to trust you?"

"Not you, Omri! Them."

Cain pointed at Jaq and then around the room at the rest of them.

Akellah rolled her eyes and tucked her gun back into its hidden holster.

"I wouldn't advise trusting this sack of shit," she huffed.

"Agreed," Kirima said, "What's your price?"

Cain smiled wide, revealing a row of sharp feline teeth. Hendrex could have sworn he saw a flash of stripes just beneath the man's skin.

"If he is here to help the Aura, I believe we should be discussing the terms," Jaq said stepping forward, but one look from Enora stopped him right in his tracks.

"I'm willing to help out, if and only if I am given free rein to court any Alulpo female in the Langsmith area."

Hendrex didn't like the sound of that or the way Akellah reached for her weapon again, only stopping when Enora placed a hand on her shoulder.

"Look this is a discussion for another time," Mack

said.

"Right, understandable. I need to make a report to Merwin so he doesn't send an army down here after me. You have three days."

With that Cain strode out of the room, taking the tension with him but leaving zero answers for all the new questions Hendrex had.

Kirima turned and glared at Jaq.

"Look son, I know you're the leader of your little Aura group, but you need to sit this one out. This is Vampire business. I've got this."

Kirima didn't bother waiting for Jaq to answer. She turned on her heels and made for the door. Carrie, Hectair, and Akellah followed her out. The room was silent for a moment as everyone attempted to process what the hell just happened.

What had started as a simple meeting about just how intertwined the three groups were in this fight had turned into an expose on the deep and twisted ancestry of the Vampire nation as a whole.

Tyr rubbed a hand over his head and shrugged.

"We'll let them handle that for now. We need time to regroup and reorganize," Donovan said.

"Fuck that! I'm not letting Vamps step in and start running shit again. No offense to Vampires present," Tyr said.

"I am inclined to agree with both of you. I don't trust the Vampires to handle themselves. They've proven on multiple occasions that they cannot be trusted to police their own. At the same time, I think we need to give Kirima a chance to weaken the forces from the inside before we make any further move. As it stands, we are too few and too vulnerable," Mack said.

"That's why we need Zazzie's school," Molly spoke up.

Hendrex could feel the shock and pride swelling in Zazzie as Molly went on about the importance of training the next generation while also providing a safe space for them while things were still tense in town. He smiled, noting how the others nodded along in agreement. Molly smiled brightly at Zazzie when she finished.

"Sorry, I didn't mean to steal your thunder, lady, but I'm just super passionate about your work. No offense to Mack, but I've learned so much from you in these last few weeks."

"No worries, I think sometimes people need to hear it from someone else for it to really sink in," Zazzie said.

Zazzie moved to the front of the room next to Tyr and Jaq.

"I do believe the school is what we need for long term success, but I'm going to need help to get it off the ground. We have the building thanks to Molly and Shane, and the curriculum I've been working on for years. The Aura Council have approved Aura students to attend, but I want this to be inclusive. I want the children to be able to learn and grow together. All these years of separation have aided in the situation we are in now. I hope to change our current trajectory with the Aura Academy," she said.

"A school where shifter kids don't have to fear accidental shifts, have space to run when needed. Sounds amazing!" Sequoia said.

Tyr's mate stood by the doorway. Her statement a surefire sign that Tyr would have no choice but to support Zazzie's school.

"I'd love to teach again, if you have room for a science teacher," Shane said.

"I could handle history, and I believe they call it shop class?" Claude said.

"Computer science for me, and all the heavy lifting

for Xander," Cat added.

"I believe my mate means weapons training," Xander clarified.

Everyone went around in a circle offering whatever services they could to help Zazzie with her school and Hendrex sat down to keep from showing how weak his knees felt in his excitement and awe of the woman who'd chosen him over all others.

Epilogue

Zazzie walked the halls of the school, admiring the work the community had done to help get the school running. Despite the show of support of her peers, it had taken months of back and forth with the Shifter Council, the Ruling Council, and the new Vampire Delegation to get the place up and running. Jasmine had done her utter best to throw a wrench in her plans, even going so far as to open a smaller program to compete with what she had already started. None of that mattered, though, because here Zazzie was, walking the halls on the very first day of school for all the Supernatural children of Langsmith. Her Aura Academy was finally a reality.

"You ready, love? The first students have arrived," Hendrex said.

Zazzie smiled widely and gave him a big hug, well, a loose hug. Her belly had gotten massive. Enora assured her it was normal for her to show so early since she was having triplets. The Andromeda penchant for multiples had managed to skip both Disrayan and Enora, and it seemed the universe was making up for it with her.

"More than ready," Zazzie said, and it was the truth.

This was the key, the final step in her journey as Zenith. With the school established and running smoothly,

Zazzie will have set the final piece in the puzzle of how the Aura were to succeed in the future. It wasn't to hide from who and what they were. It was to grow in their understanding of their abilities and their shared past with others in the Supernatural community.

"I've got the virtual classroom set up for lessons with Hectair about the Saurian. Until they have a member available to teach full time," Hendrex said.

"Nice! Akellah is staying in town. Apparently, she doesn't want to leave Keenan to his own devices. Maybe we can have her help Xander with weapons training. The man is brilliant but needs help with modernizing his methods," Zazzie pondered aloud.

Akellah had returned, bringing with her a lost text of the elders. Inside it contained the story of their origins. The original tribes who had mastered the energies and how they were preyed upon by otherworldly parasites. Those who were caught were bred to become the Saurian, and from the Saurian came what they now knew as Vampires. It was the stuff of movies and nightmares. The term Alulpo had now been added to the roster. A long-forgotten branch of the Aura. More lost ones to find and bring into the fold with the help of their new friends the Omri.

The leader of the Omri, Makai Inigo, and his mate Soulstice had arrived in person to offer their support and partnership with the Aura. Hendrex had even invited them to their Binding after bonding with Makai over a love of baseball. And despite initial tensions between the Omri and the new Vampire Delegation that was basically just Kirima, Carrie, and Molly, they'd all come to an agreement for the greater good of Langsmith and the Supernatural community as a whole. Things were far from settled, but this was a start. Today was a giant step in the right direction.

"Really? I didn't think she would stay since Hectair left," Hendrex said.

Zazzie smiled at Hendrex and his naïveté. He would assume that them being mated was the end all and be all, even after what happened between them.

"Akellah's not ready to settle down like that yet. From what I overheard when they were here for our Binding, Akellah doesn't believe Hectair's mating bond with her is real," she explained.

Hendrex's eyebrows shot up in shock.

"Maybe you should rethink her as a teacher. We need someone with good vision."

"Good vision?"

"Yes, Akellah must be blind if she can't see how absolutely obsessed Hectair is over her."

Zazzie chuckled.

"Need I remind you that obsession and even mind-blowing sex doesn't mean shit unless both parties are honest about their intentions."

Hendrex's pulled her into his arms and kissed her soundly.

"I was always honest about my intentions with you, Zazzie."

"Only after the world as you knew it ended, and I pray for everyone's sake that doesn't need to happen for anyone else," she laughed.

"Uh, I hate to interrupt, but we have a small problem in the science lab," Shane said.

"I'll handle it. You go greet the students," Hendrex said.

He kissed her cheek, and then her belly, before disappearing with Shane down the hall to the STEM Lab. A smile on her face, Zazzie made her way to the front of the building. The wide wooden doors were already propped open, but Enora had helped Zazzie erect an energy shield that blocked any uninvited guests from entering beyond that point. There was a smaller glass door off to the side as a public entrance to the school; a funnel point for any visitors not in the know.

With a deep breath, Zazzie stepped out to greet the anxious parents and students.

"Welcome to Aura Academy!" she announced.

More From Stella Williams

Paranormal Romance & Urban Fantasy

<u>Maura's Men Trilogy</u>

Xander's Claim
Claude's Conquest
Shane's Redemption

<u>Secret of Ceres Series</u>

Ferocious
Dauntless
Earnest
Zenith

<u>Langsmith Shifter Shorts</u>

Coy Wolf
A Night Divine
Bird of Prey

<u>Bloodlines</u>

His Soul to Keep

Contemporary Romance

<u>Paramour Novellas</u>

Felling Bechet
Unforgettable Valentine

About the Author

Stella Williams is a Blogger and USA TODAY Bestselling Paranormal Romance & Urban Fantasy Author, who lives in Washington State. She has a degree in Anthropology from The University of California, Santa Cruz. Stella prides herself in using her studies to create diverse worlds and characters for her novels.

You can find more about Stella Williams on her website: www.serpentinecreative.com

Want More of Stella's Seductive Supernatural World? Keep up to date with Stella Williams and her latest projects.

https://serpentinecreative.com/links